I0681236

A DARK FICTION LITERARY ANTHOLOGY

Volume 8

Guest Edited by
Tamela J. Ritter

Dark Alley Press

INK STAINS ANTHOLOGY
Volume 8

ISBN 13: 978-1-946050-09-0

Dark Alley Press
http://www.darkalleypress.com

An imprint of Vagabondage Press LLC
PO Box 3563
Apollo Beach, Florida 33572
http://www.vagabondagepress.com

First edition printed in the United States of America and the United Kingdom, April 2018

10 9 8 7 6 5 4 3 2 1

Front cover photo by Simon Wijers.

INK STAINS

A DARK FICTION LITERARY ANTHOLOGY

TABLE OF CONTENTS

INTRODUCTION

When I was first asked to be a Guest Editor for *Ink Stains*, I was leery. Being a skittish kitten about blood and guts, about monsters and things that creep and crawl, I was terrified about what I'd be exposing myself to by curating a collection. But I like to challenge myself, push against my comforts, and most importantly, I like coming across and discovering stories that surprise me, that take me on a journey.

So, I took a deep breath and started reading through the submissions. And yes, some of the things I found pushed against the comfort zone a disturbing amount, but more than that, they surprised me, delighted me, and took me on a journey—literally. The stories I have found for you are told on a map of the world. We find the adage *revenge is a dish best served cold* is true in India; *true love survives anything*, even tragedy, in New Zealand. We visit a mysterious forest in France during WW1 and a working ranch in the American West. Also, just for fun, we get into the mind of a psychotic slasher at a summer camp.

And yes, there is cannibalism and zombies and even creepy, crawly things, but there is also finding second chances out of dead-end jobs at the very rock bottom and the dark, dangerous addiction that comes with finally getting your dream come true.

I have had a surprisingly good time finding these unique slices of a life that none of us would ever want to live, but we'll all enjoy visiting. I hope you discover things that make you think, make you feel, and yes, make your skin crawl. Don't worry though, I also included a few gems that will make you laugh. I promise.

Tamela J. Ritter
Guest Editor
Ink Stains Anthology

THE ROACHES RESPOND

Kevin Roller

It was perched on the edge of the table, dark brown and gleaming. Anton stopped, midstride, at the sight of the thumb-sized creature. It was motionless except for its twitching antennae, each of which moved with an unsettling lack of synchronicity. He blinked, and the bug scuttled over the edge, beneath the table, out of sight.

Was that a cockroach? Anton thought, though he knew from the spreading feeling of disgust in his stomach that the answer was yes.

What had the cockroach crawled over? Which papers? Which chisels? Anton thought of its legs, hairy and unclean, moving with frenetic speed over his possessions. He stroked his beard but then stopped. Had he used that hand to touch anything on the table? He left the studio and went into the bathroom, where he washed his hands with six pumps of soap. He then scrubbed his beard, using eight pumps of soap, for good measure.

As he worked the last of the suds out of his beard, Anton thought: *Even if your hand did touch something the bug had been on, there's no way it would have contaminated your beard.* It was just a bug, after all; some people in the world even eat cockroaches, like they were popcorn or pork rinds. But still, he remembered those hairy legs running across his table, covered in indelible and diffusive germs…

Once his face was dry, Anton returned to his studio. The room was littered with chisels, hammers, models, and posters of Rodin's and Michelangelo's sculptures. A block of marble the size of a refrigerator towered over the room, raised on a metal platform. Anton was carving the figure of a woman from the block; smooth, spindly arms hung above her head while the bottom half of her body waded, unreleased, in the anonymous stone. Anton thought that statues looked most beautiful this way—human faces and limbs and torso melting, ghostlike, out of the ether.

Anton had been commissioned to construct this sculpture by a man named Jacobs Westling. Jacobs said he was a banker, but Anton didn't need to be told that; he had been to enough art galas and museum fundraisers to know how wealth carried itself: pedantic, fastidious, knowing. Anton had had several sculptures requested (and handsomely paid for) by the art-world genteel. He noticed that the younger men wanted statues of their women, wives or mistresses, while the older men wanted busts of themselves. *I bet they see themselves as conquerors, like the Romans; it's only natural that they would want to be commemorated in the same way,* Anton thought. He did it for the money; there was no disputing that. While he was in art school, Anton told himself that he would never work for money alone, that only his muse and his chisel would guide him. It wasn't long after graduation that he realized what a trite cliché he was: selling one statue to the MET didn't pay the rent, nor did it buy girls drinks or pay for fresh blocks of marble. He felt dirty at first, though the sensation was alleviated by the growing number in his checking account. He would occasionally think back to that young idealist, the would-be starving artist (with no idea of what that entailed), and wondered if that younger him would be repulsed by current him; knowing the answer, Anton deposited every hefty check he received almost immediately after he received it.

Jacobs wanted Anton to sculpt his daughter, an aspiring ballet dancer named Agatha. Anton's original suggestions for the sculpture were more conservative, parent-friendly: mostly of a thin woman pirouetting or stretching. These did not appeal to Jacobs.

"These don't do anything for me. Maybe they're good for another girl, someone more diffident and passive, but not Agatha," the banker said. "Make her look like a Greek goddess, with the power of Athena and the grace of Aphrodite. She is powerful for her size, flawless and fierce. There's no way to encapsulate her spirit in anything that isn't massive, intimidating, and marble."

He made several more suggestions, posing the dancers in more exaggerated and violent stances, but nothing he suggested seemed to intrigue Jacobs. Close to three hours later, Anton, frustrated and wanting to shock the bastard, drafted another model of Agatha, still pirouetting but only covering her body with a thin tutu. Anton knew that he was effectively screwing himself out of a paycheck, but he didn't care. *This guy isn't worth the headache,* he thought. Jacobs clearly needed reminding that *Anton* was the artist — that *Anton* had the talent — that *he* wore the smock dappled with crusted clay and that Jacobs wore the stiff, dark suit.

It's good money, Anton told himself every time he picked up the chisel. *It's good money,* every time he consulted the clay model. *It's good money,* every time he thought of Jacobs's eyes lighting up when Anton showed him the crude sketch. Jacobs withdrew his checkbook and scratched out several zeros, his eyes flitting from the sketch to the check feverishly. *Do you know how many sculptors would kill for a check like that?* Jacobs grinned unctuously as he mentioned a bonus (if he liked what he saw when the job was done). He ran his tongue over yellow teeth. *It's good money.*

Anton willed himself to stop thinking about Jacobs, and about the hidden but surely present cockroach, as he went back to work. Today he was shaping on one of her plump but firm deltoids. It was a difficult muscle to craft: too big and she looked like a roided-out bodybuilder; too small and she looked ineffably flimsy.

He felt something squirm under his palm. Anton dropped his chisel in shock—a brown bug was moving up his sleeve. It was fast, way too fast, crawling up his arm, nearing his shoulder. He let out a gasp and swatted at the bug, hitting *something* (the bug felt like nothing, as if he had smacked a piece of plastic), and the bug was gone. He scoured the floor in the direction he had hit the roach, but he could not find it. Had he killed it? He didn't think so; there was no organic debris on his shirt or hand to suggest that.

A sickening brand of adrenaline filled him; everything around him seemed stained with invisible shit and malicious germs. He tugged off his shirt and threw it toward his laundry basket as he walked into the bathroom. Anton scrubbed his arms up to the shoulder, and (*just in case*, he thought) washed his face and beard again.

* * * *

Anton felt that the small, enclosed world of his apartment had been tainted. He wasn't sure of the exact moment when the bugs went from a minor nuisance to an overwhelming infestation. Their arrival was like the tipping point in May, when the warmth of the spring boiled over into sweltering, oppressive summer. They were on his shelves, scuttling over his sketchbooks, spreading their germs over virgin surfaces. He found three roaches nuzzling under a chicken breast just off the skillet. He could see them rushing into various cracks in the wall or seams in the wainscoting as he entered a room, though some would freeze in place either oblivious, overwhelmed by, or ambivalent of his presence. Some of the bugs even mounted the statue, surrounding Agatha's white face or dotting the small of her back.

He had trouble sleeping after a cockroach swiftly crawled over his face; its dull-needle legs grazed his lips. He vomited. In a rage, Anton grabbed his hammer from the studio and began smashing holes in his wall, chasing shadows that could have been the offending roach.

His skin was becoming dry and irritated with the constant application of soap and water. After the chicken breast incident, Anton started washing all of his silverware and plates before using them.

Three more days, Anton thought. *Three more days until the exterminator gets here and nukes the fuckers.* Anton tried to call the exterminator the night that the bug had crawled across his face but reached only a voicemail. He realized he was irrationally angry that they did not answer, given that it was one in the morning, but he was angry nonetheless. He stayed up all that night, chasing cockroaches with his rubber hammer, listening to the sickening crunch of their tiny bodies under its face. When he did reach the exterminator's office, several frustrating hours after the sun had risen, the receptionist told him that the soonest they could get someone to his studio wasn't for another week. He began silently weeping.

"Seven days with these goddamn bugs?" he moaned, rebuking himself later for his maudlin and pathetic tone.

The receptionist, whom Anton pictured as an old woman, wearing half-moon glasses over a thin face, said: "New York's a big city filled with bugs. You think you're the only one who can't stand 'em?"

Two more days. Agatha's legs were now free; the sculpture was almost complete. The night before, he had accidentally smashed his clay model, which he made of Agatha when she came to his studio. She was small and narrow with an assured but obstinate look in her eye. He had seen the same look in the eyes of her father, in rapacious old men with young escorts propped up beside them, in perfidious wives who lead him by the hand into unoccupied bathrooms and coat closets. This look inculcated by unrestricted sexuality, too much money, and a general but passive lack of humanity.

Anton did not have sex with Agatha, though he was almost positive that he could have; he felt the tip of her breast brush against him while he posed her, and the look in her eye after it happened told him that it was intentional. *It's good money.* She held still for several hours as he made a rough model out of clay, which would serve as a template for the sculpture itself. When he had finished, Anton felt that he was looking at the statue of a girl instead of a woman. He noticed how small she looked, vulnerable, except for her eyes, as she pulled her sweater back on. Anton was suddenly ashamed to have scrutinized her naked body so closely.

Now the model was a smattering of brown blades. The bugs scuttled over the shards; he thought they were mocking him.

Every night, as the sun went down, as the bugs emerged from unidentified cracks in the wall or holes in the floor, as Anton's fruitless and unending slaughter of the roaches began, he saw yellow. Seeing red was a common platitude, Anton knew, used to describe the uncontrollable rage soldiers felt in the heat of battle (or by a murderer pleading temporary insanity on the stand). But, during his own battle, Anton felt nothing but unhinged disgust and revulsion; the color he saw was that of puss, rotten corn, dead grass, stained and savage teeth.

* * * *

The bugs were drawn to the statue. It wasn't a conclusion he reached after protracted contemplation, but something he knew in his gut, like knowing when someone was watching you. They would roam over her eyes or between her shoulder blades, dark brown splotches sickeningly juxtaposed with her marble skin. At half past one in the morning, through the thick fog of disgust and sleeplessness, Anton thought he saw the bugs forming on the statue's face, one over each eye and several across her lips, antennae twitching but otherwise still. It looked like a crude, broken smile. He shook his head and the bugs had broken their formation, though still lingered on her face. *You're losing your shit,* Anton thought. Then he thought, *It's good money.*

Heavy knocks on his door brought Anton out of a thin sleep. He had passed out in his bathtub, surrounded by pesticides and rubber gloves. He thought about leaving, about heading to a hotel or motel or anywhere, but he did not; for some reason, it felt traitorous to leave the statue, so near completion, alone with the cockroaches. He called the landlord at 3:35 a.m. to complain. The landlord, his voice thick with sleep, told him that no one else in the building had seen any bugs. When Anton started screaming as he flicked a roach off his pants, the landlord said he would come by first thing in the morning ("In the *actual* morning, not now," the landlord said) to investigate. If he found Anton's claims to be true, he would pay for the exterminator. He looked at his watch now, rubbing the sleep from his eyes; it was 4:26, just a few minutes before sunrise.

"It's about time," Anton said as he opened the door. "I haven't killed any in a few hours, but—"

Jacobs Westling was on the other side of the door.

"Killed what?" Jacobs asked, his voice high and whining.

"Nothing really," Anton stammered. "I've just, well, I've been having a bit of, uh…"

Would Jacobs really understand? Jacobs had probably never encountered actual filth, the kind that feels like it's underneath your fingernails or burrowing into your pores. *Crossing the threshold into my apartment might be the closest he'll ever come,* Anton thought, forcing down the yellow feeling as he gestured Jacobs inside.

"I hope you don't mind my dropping in. I just wanted to check on my investment," Jacobs said, pulling off his leather gloves. He was looking at the statue. Anton prayed that, for once, there were no bugs on it. "I was on my way to the airport; the jet *insists* on leaving at the crack of dawn."

"No, no trouble at all," Anton said. *If it were any trouble, you'd never know*, Anton thought, wondering how much unconscious trouble Jacobs had caused in his life. "I only have to finish her feet and then the statue will be ready. Maybe another two or three days."

But Jacobs did not appear to be listening; his body was still, arrested in front of the statue. His eyes were wide, and his mouth was ajar, displaying his crooked, yellow teeth.

"Mr. Westling?" Anton said, and Jacobs started, as if a trance had been broken.

"Would you mind," Jacobs said, looking embarrassed, pulling his trench coat shut, "would you mind pouring me a cup of coffee? I'm feeling a little bit tired."

Anton hesitated and then nodded.

As he thoroughly washed two coffee cups in the kitchen, waiting for the coffee brewer to warm up, Anton watched Jacobs Westling out of the corner of his eye. Jacobs was circling the statue, his eyes moving up and down its alabaster form. Two bugs dashed across his counter; Anton stealthily managed to crush one of them with the bottom of a clean mug while the other got away. Jacobs was running his fingertips across the statue's ankles as he walked, still circling slowly, quiet and reverential. Anton scraped the bug's carcass off the bottom of the mug with a paper towel; the cockroach was mostly whole, though greenish puss leaked from its cracked shell. Jacobs's palm glided over her thighs as he continued to circle.

It's good money.

The brewer chirped. Anton put the paper towel on his counter, next to the defiled mug. He was watching Jacobs directly. Jacobs's hands were moving up and down the statue's frozen body.

It's good money.

Anton thought of Agatha: she looked so small in the streets, so vulnerable. She probably knew why the statue had been commissioned, and why it had to be nude. Maybe he had misunderstood that defiant look in her eye; perhaps it was not inspired by spoiled, wealthy selfishness but was a defense mechanism, her intimidation and forwardness akin to an octopus turning garish colors to ward off the predator. Jacobs was a wealthy man, but by no means an alpha-male dripping with testosterone; Jacobs was tepid, pusillanimous, Nero as opposed to Caesar. This defense of Agatha's would ward off Jacobs, too vibrant and aggressive for her predator. But not anymore: she was approachable, touchable, trapped in stone and defenseless against her own father's lusting.

As he watched Jacobs surreptitiously slide his hand beneath the stone tutu, Anton scrapped the roach carcass off the paper towel (*It's good money*) into the sodden mug, and filled the mug with hot coffee.

But was it unwitting? Anton thought as he left the kitchen. *Didn't you always know why he wanted the statue? You did; you know you did. You just kept your eyes on the money, like you always do, and tried not to think about it. What kind of an artist does that? The bugs wouldn't allow it. Maybe they wanted to show you.*

Jacobs jumped back from the statue, his hands snapping to his sides, when Anton returned, but Anton feigned ignorance; he smiled at Jacobs, though the world began to turn yellow.

"Thank you," Jacobs said as he accepted the cup. "It's really marvelous what you've created here. It's exactly what I wanted. I feel that this really captures Agatha's mien. Do you understand? Of course you do; you met her after all. Is she not intoxicating?"

"Your daughter?" Anton asked, wanting to twist the knife just a bit.

"Well, yes, my daughter," Jacobs said, appearing to choke on the last word.

Anton hesitated and said, "Yes, she's really something."

The pair stared at the statue in silence. Anton's eye flitted back between the steaming mug in Jacobs's hands and the statue, the mug and the statue, the mug and the statue. He thought he felt something small crawl over his shoe but did not look down. Jacobs's eyes had grown wide again, like full moons, as the decorum of conversation faded. The bugs began to appear in Anton's peripheral vision, on his tables and on the floor.

"You know," Jacobs said, "when I was a boy, I wanted to be an artist, too. I used to paint landscapes and the occasional nude; the maids were unwilling to pose, at first, but I paid well. But no, my daddy wanted me to take up the family helm. Maybe if he had another son, one with a penchant for the world of finance, I could have run off to paint. What's a wealthy family without a few eccentrics? There wasn't another son, unfortunately, so I abandoned art."

Jacobs paused and took a sip from his coffee. Anton clenched his teeth. The bugs were everywhere now, their germs contaminating everything. In his mind, he could see them ripping the top off the pesticides bottle and guzzling its contents, laughing drunkenly. They were procreating, on the spot, just out of sight, their crawling progeny emanating yellow dust in their wake. He fought the overwhelming desire to grab his hammer, to wash his hands until there was no skin left to be dirty.

"Yes, I abandoned it," Jacobs continued. "I went to the finest business schools and developed an impressive business acumen myself. I followed the money throughout my father's company: it would jump from one company to the next, cross borders, disappear entirely and then reappear, fortified and bulkier. It was a feat, but I always felt the call of the artist in my heart. When I look at works like this, I know why. I know—I see that…"

Jacobs trailed off. His face contorted; he made strange puckering noises with his mouth. Anton watched Jacobs pull his eyes off the statue for the first time since he arrived and glowered at the contents, looking for the source of distaste. Seconds later, he saw it: broken shell, drenched antennae, floating burnt and black in the coffee. Jacobs dropped his mug and screamed.

"*Finally!*" Anton yelled feverishly, scrambling for his hammer. "Don't you see them now? Do you finally see?"

Jacobs fell backward, terrified by the sight of Anton clutching his hammer. He dry-heaved on the ground. A stream of coffee flowed toward him from the shattered mug. "What the fuck is wrong with you?" Jacobs said.

"*Me?* What's wrong with *me?* I saw you, Jacobs Westling. I saw you fondling the statue of your own daughter."

Jacobs stopped retching and stared at Anton, like a child caught urinating in his grandmother's garden.

"You're-you're fucking *fired!*" Jacobs yelled.

Anton started to howl with laughter, tightening his grip on the hammer.

"Excellent news! Perfect! I've been surrounded by filth ever since I took on this project, including this very moment. Do you still not see them? Look around, Jacobs; look at the filth you've drawn here."

Jacobs looked around and screamed again, this time jumping to his feet. Cockroaches mottled every visible surface, moving with unnatural speed toward the statue. Anton turned to see them mounting her feet, en masse, crawling up her thighs and over her tutu. The figure became a brown, seething mass in seconds, sickeningly gleaming under the fluorescent lights.

Jacobs rushed for the door; Anton did not stop him. He knew, with the same sense that told him the statue was their beacon, that Jacobs's role in this had ended, that what came next could be done by him alone.

He opened his tool drawer and pulled out his largest chisel. All was tinged yellow in his revulsion. Anton leveled the chisel over the statue's heart and, as bugs climbed down its length and onto Anton's arm, he brought the hammer down on its end. The chisel pierced the wall of bugs, sending green fluid and white dust in all directions. He kept smashing, bringing the hammer down onto the end of the chisel's handle over and over again, driving the chisel deeper and deeper into the statue. His arms felt wet; he felt tiny feet feverishly scuttling over his bare skin. He continued to hammer. The chisel ate deeper and deeper into the body of the sculpture until the rock itself began to groan. The bugs, sensing what was going to happen next, began crawling off the figure, moving in waves from the top down, or fell in large, hellish clumps from her form. Anton drove the chisel further. The top half of her body slid off the rest, splitting from her left shoulder to right side. Anton, drenched in yellow and blind to all else, did not feel her stone head collided with his. The world snapped from yellow to black.

Dry, granular air was sucked into his body. Anton felt an immense weight moved off his chest; he began to cough violently as dust clung to his mouth and throat. He felt anonymous hands on his body, lifting him. He was then gently placed on something long and semi-elastic. The darkness dissipated slowly, and the picture came into view clearly: his landlord, portly and red-faced, was staring at the shattered torso of Agatha; several firemen wiped white dust off of their gloves and heavy yellow jackets; a bald man wearing a jumpsuit and what appeared to be a flamethrower was staring at Anton; the handlebars of the stretcher, on which he had been placed, and the faces of three bored-looking EMTs. Jacobs was not there.

"How is he?" his landlord asked the EMTs.

"Okay," one of them answered. "A little banged up, but okay. Looks like he's a bit more conscious. We'll know more once we get him to the hospital—"

"I'm leaving," the bald man interrupted. "I haven't found a single goddam bug in this place. I've looked in every corner, behind every piece of furniture, under every piece of rock, but I haven't seen anything."

Anton tried to sit up, to refute the man he now realized was the exterminator, but he could not move; he was bound to the stretcher with thick, red straps.

"What is it, Anton? What is it?" his landlord asked.

"We need to get him out of here, too much stress right now," said an EMT.

"Yes, of course," the landlord said. "Anton isn't the type to just make up a cockroach infestation," he added, now addressing the exterminator. "You should have heard him when we spoke last night. He sounded terrified."

"I think I get the idea," the exterminator responded. "He scared the living shit out of my secretary, sounded like a goddam lunatic she said."

"Christ. You're sure you didn't find *anything*?"

EMTs began pushing the stretcher toward the door. Anton thrashed in his restraints; he saw a tiny cockroach, no bigger than a thumbtack, crawl over the statue's ear and then disappear from sight.

"No, I couldn't find a goddam thing."

XOXOX XOXOX XOXOX X

About the Author

Kevin Roller is a writer of horror, mystery, and literary fiction. He lives with his wife and several unwelcome critters in Gloucester, Massachusetts.

THE SHAMBLING BLUE LINE

Michael D. Burnside

As a zombie, I have poor reflexes. And since my whole body is numb, I don't have any feel for how much pressure I'm putting on the gas or brake pedals. In other words, I really shouldn't be driving. But when I need to get from one side of the city to the other, I can either drive or shamble for a whole frigging day, so I drive.

I came up fast on a parked police cruiser. Its flashing lights bounced around the interior of my car, disorienting me, and I stomped on the brakes a few seconds too late. My tires squealed, and I slid into the cop car with a crunch.

I stumbled out of my car and looked at the damage. The front of my green Impala was pushed into the cruiser's rear end, but I could tell from the rust on the back of the cop car that the vehicle's brake lights had been smashed in some time ago.

Sergeant Andrews walked up to me, his hands on his hips. "Damn it, detective, my car is not a speed bump."

I shrugged. "Eh, that's not a bad bit of parking."

"But I get hit every time I go out!"

"Well yeah, we zombies can't drive worth shit. Tell me you didn't smack up against that curb there?"

Andrews sighed. "Don't know what we're going to do. The damage adds up. And it's not like anyone is building new cars."

"I know, but there's not much we can do about it." I pulled a pack of cigarettes out of my pocket.

"Where do you keep finding those?" asked Andrews.

I managed to fish a cigarette out of the box without mangling it. "I'm not giving up my scavenging secrets." As I fumbled with my lighter, I looked up at Andrews and noticed the tip of his nose was gone.

Sergeant Andrews hadn't been a handsome man back when he was alive. He'd always had a lopsided face and scraggly blond hair. But after he became a zombie, his beady eyes sank further into his potato-shaped head. With the loss of some of his nose, he looked downright cadaverous.

"Jesus, Andrews," I exclaimed. "What happened to your nose?"

"Oh," said Andrews. He looked down at his worn shoes. "I think a rat's been chewing on me while I sleep."

"Gotta get yourself a cat," I said.

Andrews looked up and shook his head. "A cat will eat more of me than a rat will."

"Get a zombie cat, then. They're more discriminating." I flicked my thumb against the top of my lighter. A spark flickered and died.

"Want me to help you with that?" asked Andrews.

I shook my head and flicked the lighter a half-dozen more times.

"You know, you're going to damage your thumb if you keep doing that. Then it'll fall off and you won't be able to shoot your gun."

I shrugged. "I already can't shoot worth shit. Yesterday at the range, I accidentally shot Simons. He was standing next to me when I drew my gun, and I put a slug into his leg."

Andrews snickered. "I bet he was pissed."

I shook my head. "I don't think he's noticed yet."

A flame sprang to life from my lighter. I quickly lit the end of my cigarette and managed to avoid setting my face on fire. I slipped the lighter back into my duster's pocket and forced myself to inhale.

Breathing isn't a habit for us zombies. We have to make a conscious effort to do it. Fresh zombies often try to talk without drawing in a breath. They'll stand there and wiggle their lips at you until you remind them to blow some air over their vocal chords.

Warm air flooded my lungs. Smoking makes me feel alive again. It takes the edge off of the incessant hunger. I'd quit years ago back when I was alive because I'd wanted to keep living, but now that I'm dead, fuck it. It's not going to kill me anymore dead than I already am.

I blew the smoke out of my body and watched it ascend into the sky. I turned to Officer Andrews and asked, "So why did you make me recklessly drive all the way over here?"

Andrews pointed to an apartment building with peeling red paint. Its front door had been ripped off and thrown into the street. "A mob found a human holed up in that building. She was pretty well prepared. Lots of casualties."

"Ah, crap." I took another drag on the cigarette and forced the smoke out my nose. "I've told every damn zombie I meet to leave those survivors alone. The humans that are still around are insanely dangerous."

Andrews frowned. "You know how the hunger is. One smell of fresh brains, and we lose all control."

"Hell yes, I know how the hunger is. Why do you think I smoke?"

We started walking toward the building. Its windows were boarded up but firing holes had been cut into the wood.

I stopped walking. "Crap, the human's not still in there, is she?"

Andrews shook his head. "She got out through an entrance to the roof, then ran across the top of the building and down a fire escape."

"So we don't know where she is now?"

Andrews shook his head again.

"She better not still be in there. She probably has a shotgun. I hate shotguns."

"She's long gone, Detective."

I started walking toward the apartment building again, my right foot dragging every step. I'm not sure how I hurt my foot, but it hadn't been working right for months. Once it falls off, I plan on nailing a block of wood to the resulting stump. Maybe I'll get an eye patch and start talking like a pirate.

I paused at the stairs to the apartment building and considered how ridiculous Andrews and I were, two zombies still trying to be cops.

Most zombies give up on their living professions. They wander the streets or sit in their homes watching snowy static on television. If you weren't really motivated to go to work back when you were alive, odds are against you bothering to go once you're dead. But for those of us whose lives were our professions — cops, soldiers, doctors, nurses, firefighters, etc. — a lot of us try to carry on.

I staggered up the stairs. The first body of the day was waiting for me in the doorway, a zombie dressed in a ragged business suit. His head lay in two pieces on either side of his corpse. A machete hung down from the doorframe.

"Sword trap. Nice," I muttered. I ducked under the blade and entered the apartment, stepping over the body as best I could. Officer Simons waited for us inside. He stood next to a horror show.

Officer Simons is nightmare fuel all by himself. He was one of the first infected, and he spent some time rotting in the ground before he decided to get back up and return to work. He'd lost all the hair on his head, his skin was a gross purple hue, he had no nose at all, and at some point, his lips fell off, giving him a permanent creepy, black-toothed grin. So when I say that what he stood next to was horrifying, I want you to understand my full meaning. Simons was the least disgusting thing in the room.

Next to Simons was a body pile, or perhaps I should call it a "parts pile," as none of the bodies were intact. At least fifty zombies made up the pile in a space that was no more than ten feet long and went up to the second floor. Some of the zombies still had their skulls intact and so were still animated. They thrashed around with whatever limbs they still had attached. The pile was made up of a fluid-seeping collection of torsos, legs, arms, and heads. Somewhere under the pile were the remains of a staircase.

Simons groaned at me and waved his arm at the pile.

I swore then muttered, "Jesus, I haven't seen anything like this since the Fall."

Andrews nodded, stepped past me, and pointed at a wooden plank on the bottom of the pile. "What Simons is trying to say is that the human destroyed the staircase. The mob piled in and stacked up, one on top of the other. When, the pile got high enough to reach the second floor, the human set off an improvised explosive."

Andrews pointed to a perforated zombie head near the bottom of the pile. "She packed the bomb with deck nails. She intended to inflict maximum casualties."

I pointed to one of the zombies who was still squirming. "Better than just building a pressure bomb that would blow everyone apart but leave them animated. Tell me he wouldn't have preferred a nail through the skull." I sighed. "Let's get these poor bastards out of here and do what needs to be done."

We spent the next hour pulling the pile apart. We dragged the remains into the street, tossing the completely dead into a pile and laying out the still living dead into a row on the sidewalk.

Away from the scent of fresh human brain, my fellow zombies were much more rational, some were even remorseful for trying to devour the human. I offered each of them a choice. They could try to go on existing with what was left of their bodies, or I could end their suffering with a bullet to the brain.

All but one opted for the bullet.

The one who couldn't face the end of his existence had lost half his body. I watched him hop away on one leg while he flailed his remaining arm about to maintain his balance. He fell twice as he crossed the street. I considered shooting him in the back of the head the second time, but I didn't. It was his call to make, not mine.

Andrews walked up to me and wiped his bloody hands on his pants. His uniform was a mess of stains. "I'll give Dave a call in the morning."

I nodded. Dave was a zombie who had been a construction worker back when he was alive. He still liked to play with his bulldozer. He'd helped us out before when we'd needed mass graves.

I said, "I'll drive around and make sure no new mob has gathered anywhere."

Andrews rolled his eyes at me. "What are you going to do, Vincent? We can't fight the hunger when a fresh brain is around. She's the source of the problem!"

"What am I supposed to do, arrest her for being delicious? She has every right to try to stay alive."

Andrews frowned. "As awful as it sounds, Vincent, maybe it's time to accept what we are. Maybe it's time you recognize which side you're on."

"I'm on the side that's in favor of everyone peacefully coexisting."

Andrews glanced over at the pile of body parts. "Looks like you're alone."

I dropped my cigarette and stamped on it. "Don't I fucking know it."

I marched over to my car, got in, and slammed the door shut. I turned the key, intending to drive off with an angry squealing of tires, but instead the engine whirred and died. I tried again.

Whirrrr chugga chugga chugga. Silence.

And again.

Whirrrrr chuga chugga clank. Silence.

Andrews walked over and leaned in the window. "You need a jump?"

I shook my head. "No. The ignition's just a bit tricky lately."

Whirrrr chugaa chugga. Silence.

Andrews snickered. "You know smacking into my car probably didn't help it any."

"Yeah. Yeah."

Whirrr chugga chugga. Vroom!

"Got it!" I motioned Andrews away. "Mind stepping back? I had this whole 'drive off angry' scenario planned."

Andrews nodded. "Sure. Try not to hit my car again though, okay? And please don't hit the body pile. If you get stuck in that, I'm not pushing you out of it."

"I'll do my best."

I put the car in reverse, backed away from Andrew's car and flattened a No Parking sign. I stomped on the accelerator and pulled off a decent half-donut, complete with smoking tires. I jumped the curb on the other side of the street, missed a fire hydrant by inches, and ran over a Stop sign. I got the car onto the street again and sped off into the setting sun.

I spent the next few hours driving around looking for any signs of a human holding off a mob of zombies. All I managed to find was a zombie who'd gotten his head stuck in a bucket. After I rescued him, I headed home.

Zombies don't really sleep, though we do enjoy a bit of quiet downtime during which we actually act like the corpses we are and stop moving around. I spent the night lying in bed and overthinking things.

If any of the zombies in the mob had managed to bite the human, the whole crisis would resolve itself. She'd be a zombie by morning. That's the way it works.

If a horde of zombies succeeds in eating a human's brains, then the human dies and goes off to whatever afterlife there may be. But holding someone down and devouring them alive is no easy task. The person being eaten tends to object rather strenuously and often gets away. If they get away but get bitten in the process, they end up becoming one of us, the living dead.

Being a zombie has some advantages. You don't feel pain. You don't have to eat. Things that used to kill you, like drowning, aren't really a problem anymore. But the downsides are huge. You don't feel much in the way of pleasure. You're always hungry, but only fresh human brains have any flavor, and there's some uncomfortable moral problems with getting those. And any damage your body incurs never gets better. Eventually, we zombies just fall apart.

In many ways, the world reflects what we are. Without dexterous, motivated humans to care for it, civilization is decaying. Eventually all the cars will stop running. The bridges will fall into the rivers. The nuclear power plant on the hill will fail.

Maybe the resulting radiation will tickle.

If bitten, the woman would go from being a living person to a shambling corpse like me. Something precious would be lost, and there still dwelled within me a tiny spark that didn't want that to happen.

Whoever she was, she was a survivor. She'd managed to make it through the last year of carnage. She could fight. She could build bombs and traps, so she had mechanical aptitude. She'd planned an escape route. She was probably ex-military. Odds were good she was still alive.

My phone rang just as the first rays of the morning sun broke through my window. Cells phones were sketchy at this point, but a lot of the old landlines still worked. I mumbled a hello into the receiver. The caller responded with a groaning that sounded like a soul being tortured in hell.

"Simons, is that you?" I asked.

"Mraugghhh! Aurgughha!"

"Simons, put Andrews on the phone."

"Aurughha Ra!"

"Yes, now!"

Fuck, I feel sorry for the guy, but once your damn lips fall off, it's time to let others do the talking.

Andrews must have snatched the phone because the next voice yelling at me was his. "She's in the damn police station!"

"Who's in the what now?"

"The human," said Andrews. "She got into the precinct. A mob is forming up outside!"

"I'll be right there." I hung up the phone and rolled out of bed. I hadn't changed out of my clothes last night, hadn't even taken my shoes off. I felt like crap.

"How the fuck am I supposed to do mornings without coffee?"

I patted my pocket. I still had cigarettes, but it was my last pack, and I had a feeling I was going to need all the ones I had today.

I lurched toward the front door, passing by the temptation to stop in the bathroom and look in the mirror. The last time I had checked, I was looking pretty good for a zombie. Most of my straw-colored hair was still in place. My eyes had looked a little glassy, but were still blue. My skin was a bit pallid but hadn't started to rot. I could almost pass as human, but I knew that wouldn't last.

It took a full minute of key turning before my Impala started. In my rush to back out of my driveway, I hit my mailbox leaving it sticking out of the ground at an odd angle.

The zombie who is my mail carrier sometimes still does his route, but since he doesn't have any letters to deliver, he just stuffs the mailboxes with things he finds.

It's usually roadkill.

I shoved the gear stick forward and stomped on the accelerator. The Impala lurched forward and tore through my neighbor's yard, spitting out dead grass behind it. I steered the rampaging machine onto the street and headed toward the station.

I may have sideswiped an abandoned car or two on the way, but I managed to arrive at the precinct. A mob of zombies was trying to shove themselves through the front door. Andrew's police cruiser was parked a way off from the crowd. I parked behind the station to avoid smashing into his car or accidentally plowing through the mob.

I limped all the way to the front of the building, past the mob, and up to officers Simons and Andrews. They stared at the mob with their jaws slightly agape.

"Not joining in the rampaging?" I asked. "Good for you."

Simons moaned something. Andrews shook his head, looked at his feet, and said, "I'm going to need to move back further soon. The smell of her…All I want to do is run in there and tear her skull open. The only thing keeping me in the check is the memory of that body pile she created yesterday. I don't want to go out like that."

As soon as Andrews mentioned the smell, I noticed it too. A spicy, sweet odor that somehow snuck around the rotting rank of Simons' decaying flesh.

Simons moaned again and took a step toward the mob. He stopped himself from going any further by grabbing onto the fender of Andrew's cruiser and curling his fingers into the wheel well.

"Why's the smell bothering him?" I asked. "He doesn't even have a nose."

Andrews looked up. "The olfactory bulb is located inside the skull." The expression on my face must have conveyed my lack of comprehension, because he quickly added, "The nose just gathers the smell. The brain is what detects it." He pointed at my face. "With that intact honker of yours, it should be hitting you worse than either of us."

I sighed and nodded. The longer I stood there, the stronger the pull of the odor became.

I looked at the mob crushing themselves through the front door. They were doing considerable damage to themselves by trying to enter six or seven at a time. I watched a woman in a paisley dress get her arm ripped clean off on the doorframe.

Maybe I could somehow crawl over top of them and get inside. Then I could find the woman, smash her skull open, and feast upon the warm gooey treasure within.

The sound of a shotgun blast snapped me back to my senses. Three or four more loud bangs followed. The mob outside didn't seem deterred, but I knew within the station several zombies had just gotten their insides painted onto the walls.

"She must have been low on ammunition," I said, mostly to myself. "Figured the police station would be a good place to rearm."

"There might be a box of shells left," said Andrews, "but we pretty much burned through all the shotgun ammo back when this whole mess started." He frowned. "Course we were on the other side back then."

His comment cut at me. I frowned and shook my head. "No. We're still on the side of law and order. And that mob doesn't look at all orderly." I marched toward the mob.

Andrews called after me. "You can't disperse that mob! And if you get too close, you'll join it!"

I stopped. Both were valid points.

How was I supposed to convince a bunch of brain-hungry zombies to go home? Pepper spray is only mildly irritating to us. The smell of brains is the only scent that gets our attention. Fire would work. The threat of being burned seems to kick in enough self-preservation instinct to send most zombies scattering. But I didn't really want to hurt anyone in the mob. They couldn't help themselves. And setting the precinct on fire wouldn't help the human any either.

I glanced at the back of the station. No one was there. Brain-lust had short-circuited the logic centers in the hungry mob and none of them had thought to try the back door.

I walked toward the back of the station and Andrews' second point started to become an issue. The closer I got to the woman, the more I could smell her, and the more I felt the urge to frenzy. I'd been in the area too long already. The odor receptors in my brain were becoming saturated

I made sure I wasn't breathing and climbed up the back steps. Odors can apparently float right up your nose though, because I could still smell her.

I fumbled with the keys a bit, but got the back door unlocked. I started to open it but recalled the sword trap the human had set up the last time she was surrounded. I cracked the door and peeked in. Sure enough, there was a wire attached to the door handle on the other side. I pulled out my lighter and, after a few flicks, burned the wire.

I opened the door. Inside the door frame was an old pistol angled for a head shot.

I shambled down the hall toward the sound of fighting, toward the smell. The odor caused my head to spin. I caught myself opening my mouth to inhale the sweet air and let loose a howl of desire.

I didn't draw in a breath. I clamped my mouth shut. Sucking the odor in would make the effect ten times worse. The condition fed itself, caused its victims to take actions that made it intensify.

I figured if I kept analyzing what was happening to me, I could distract myself enough to lessen its hold on me. This actually worked pretty well. I made it past the back holding cells. Then I rounded a corner, and there she was.

She had short black hair that would pass military regulations, but it was uneven in the back. She must have been cutting it herself. She was only average in height but powerfully built with strong biceps that pressed tight against the green army T-shirt she wore. An empty pistol holster was tied to her right ankle. A shotgun lay on the floor, its ejection port open.

The woman had her shoulder pressed up against a door at the end of the hallway. Her legs strained to hold her position against a horde of zombies threatening to swarm through. One of the zombies had succeeded in getting his hand past the doorframe. Long thin fingers with torn flesh that revealed bone curled around the door.

I charged down the corridor and slammed into the door which neatly amputated the fingers of the zombie who had been threatening to get through.

I felt a little bad about it.

My appearance startled the woman. She backed off, and the mob of zombies on the other side of the door succeeded in shoving the door open an inch. "Push! Push!" I yelled as my shoes slipped on the tile floor. The woman threw her weight against the door again, and we managed to get it closed. I twisted the lock shut.

I'd inhaled when I yelled for the woman to help close the door. The full force of her scent hit me. I imagined turning around, scooping her eyeballs from her skull, and then pulling her brain out through the sockets. Instead, I put my forehead up against the metal door and slid down to the floor.

"Where'd you come from?" asked the woman. "Did you get bit on your way in?"

"I got bit some time ago," I answered. Another wave of the woman's scent hit me. I felt dizzy. "Ah, Jesus," I muttered and rolled over. She saw my face. I must not have looked as good as I thought I did, because she immediately reached down and grabbed the shotgun.

"Ah fuck," I moaned. "Not the shotgun."

"It's empty," she said. "I'm going to have to beat you to death with it."

"Well that sucks." I wondered if I'd have time for a last smoke. Probably not, but I reached into my pocket and pulled out my last pack anyway. Trying to get one lit might take my mind off the beating that was to come.

She raised the butt end of the shotgun over my head and said, "I hate smokers."

I nodded. "Me too." I pulled a cigarette free of the pack but squished it pretty bad. I put it in my mouth. The end of it drooped low.

The woman didn't bring the butt of the shotgun down onto my head. Instead she said, "You're the first zombie I could ever understand."

"Well, I still have my lips. That helps a lot." I was trying to be funny, thinking that perhaps my charm might save me, but it felt like I was having a conversation with a delicious piece of steak. I pulled out my lighter. Smoking always helped keep the hunger at bay, but my hands shook as I tried to light it.

"Tell you what, since you aren't trying to kill me, if you don't light that damn cigarette, I won't smash your brains in," said the woman.

"But I need this cigarette." My voice cracked. My hands shook as I uselessly flicked the lighter. I was losing control. I was just moments away from flinging myself at her. "It'll help with the hunger, maybe drive away the smell."

"What smell?"

"The smell of your brain." I fumbled with the lighter and dropped it. I resigned myself to my fate. "Fuck it. Just kill me before I do something I'll hate myself for."

The woman picked up the lighter. Her thumb flicked the lighter with a single strong stroke and a flame burst into being. I never thought I'd think having strong thumbs would be sexy, but damn if it wasn't in that moment.

She lit the end of my damaged cigarette. "My name's Ann."

I inhaled and glorious warmth flooded my body. The smell of burning tobacco crowded out the alluring spiciness of Ann's brain. "Hi Ann. I'm Vincent."

Ann sat down, though she kept one hand on the shotgun. "Vincent, why are you different from the other zombies?"

I took another long drag from the cigarette and tried my best to exhale away from her. "Not different really. Maybe a little better willpower. Maybe worse willpower, given the smoking habit. I dunno. But most of us are fairly reasonable until we get near a living human."

Ann motioned at the door. "You mean all those crazed lunatics trying to devour me are just like you?"

I nodded. "Yeah. Until they get a whiff of you. Then some insane zombie instinct kicks in. But otherwise, we're all just normal people." I thought about that for a second and winced. "Okay, maybe normal is stretching it a bit."

The mob thumped on the door. I thumped back. "Simmer down!" I looked at Ann. "They won't listen…"

"So what now?" asked Ann.

"The back door is probably still clear. I got a car parked outside. If we can get it started, we can drive out of here."

Ann peered at me. "And how far can I trust you?"

I patted my coat pocket. "I still have at least a half-pack. I'm good for the next hour or so."

We made it out the back of the building without running into any zombies, though I tripped, fell down the back steps, and face planted. Ann helped me to my feet by hauling me up by the collar of my coat.

"Are you all right?"

I shrugged. "Hardly felt a thing." I limped toward my green Impala. "Listen, you should probably drive."

The car wouldn't start, of course, which made our dramatic get-away substantially less dramatic. Ann opened the hood and fiddled with the spark plugs while I radioed Andrews.

"Hey, I got her out."

"What?"

"The girl, I got her out of the building. We snuck out the back. Can you keep the mob focused on the front of the building till we get my car started?"

Andrews didn't seem to believe me. "How the hell are you not tearing her apart?"

"Cigarettes," I answered. "They're a lifesaver."

Andrews snorted and then said, "I'll see what I can do."

A moment later, Ann got back in the car and gave me a puzzled look. "I swore I heard a cop shouting 'Nothing to see here! Move along!'"

"Yeah, that's my buddy, Andrews."

She raised an eyebrow. "A zombie cop?"

"Yeah."

"This has turned into a weird day." She turned the key, and the Impala rumbled to life.

"You're some kind of mechanical genius, aren't ya?" I asked.

Ann nodded. "I'm pretty handy."

"Would you like a job?"

I made sure the gas mask was nice and snug, opened the door, and stepped into the garage. A half-dozen zombies sat on benches in the waiting room, all wearing gas masks. It looked like a scene from some apocalyptic movie, only we'd already had our apocalypse.

I waved to them. Some of them waved back. A few had probably been waiting there for days, but when you don't need to sleep, eat, use the bathroom, and there's nothing on TV, a long wait isn't that big of a deal. They could've just come back when what they needed was ready, but I think a lot of them like hanging around with Ann. She's vibrant and funny, and with the gas masks on, there's no urge to murder her.

I walked to the back of the garage where Ann was tinkering with something inside her cage. She had a switch in there that could electrify the bars in case some zombie tried to slip in without the proper precautions. She had me touch it once to make sure it worked. By golly, it did. I now fear electricity way more than fire or shotguns.

Ann looked up at me and said, "I told you your distributor cap wouldn't be ready till Tuesday."

"I know, I just came by to see if I could borrow a pair of pliers. Oh, and I found this." I drop a can of beans I had found into the safety drawer in the cage.

Ann pulled the can out, looked at it, and scrunched up her face. "Thanks, though I'd appreciate it if you could find a survivor who was a former cook and set up a hamburger joint for me."

"I might have a lead on that, actually. We found a small camp of survivors outside of town. We've been approaching carefully, with gas masks on, tossing them cans of food."

Ann shook the can at me, "You don't make friends with canned beans."

"You do if they're hungry enough. Hey, they've stopped shooting at us when we approach."

"I want to help."

I nodded. "As soon as it gets a bit safer. They're still jumpy. We zombies can take a bullet better than you can, well generally anyway. I'm hoping to find a nuclear technician. We need to find a way to keep the lights on."

Ann nodded as she searched through a toolbox.

I asked, "Is your escort all set for when you call it a day?"

"Yeah, Andrews and Lafferty are coming by at six to walk me back to my personal fortress." Ann pulled out a pair of pliers and dropped them into the drawer. "What do you need the pliers for?"

I pulled the pliers out and clicked them open and shut a few times. "Simons found a bullet wound in his leg. I'm going to help him pull the slug out."

Ann winched. "Ouch. I hope I wasn't the one that put it there."

"Nah, that's on me." I gave Ann a smile. "But let's not share that with him. See ya, Tuesday."

XOXOX XOXOX XOXOX X

About the Author

Michael D. Burnside's previous work includes the role playing books *Baptism of Fire: World War Two Role Play* and *Space Conspiracy*. His short stories have been published by *Devolution Z Magazine*, *Outposts of Beyond*, *Youth Imagination*, and *Gathering Storm Magazine*. His latest short story, "The Burnings," is featured in the short story anthology *Beautiful Lies, Painful Truths Volume II*. Michael lives in Dayton, Ohio with lots and lots of cats. Read more nice things about him, as well as some free stories, at www.michaelburnside.com.

A Taste of Your Own Medicine

Nidhi Singh

CHANDIPORE AT SEA

It was a warm mid-March afternoon, still as death. The sea at this hour was at low tide, leaving a salty, clayish, white beach in its wake. The sun blazed down with a feverish wrath, burning the jagged black rocks that lined the embankment. Little red crabs scurried beneath the slippery boulders, seeking respite from the brilliant burst of fire coming down from the skies. Itchy mongrels sulked in the shade, panting from the heat. Little fishing boats out at sea lurked about, chasing the shades of their sails, waiting for the cool night so that they might get on with their business.

Quiet rows of small houses, shaded by plantain and coconut trees, with small fishponds upfront, lined the seashore.

Obstinate little flies, common Indian pests, swarmed over Anishta's face, ashen and twisted with pain. Sweat dried in craggy rivulets down her hollowed cheeks; strands of once shiny jet-black hair, dry and grayed now, coiled and writhed on her forehead as Valli kneeled by the charpoy and waved a frayed bamboo fan over her. It brought her little relief, as had the placebos Valli got her from the village *vaidya* — a quack with no pretense to modern medicine save a short stint as a clinic compounder where he'd measured out colorful powders and potions into newspaper wrappers or plastic bottles.

A model wife, Anishta had suddenly taken ill and, thereafter, slipped fast into delirium and stupor. Valli patiently kept pulling down the edge of her damp sari to cover the bony legs she flailed in pain. Their daughter, unattended and forgotten until she wailed, crawled nearby on the cow dung-plastered courtyard, pushing out a little wooden toy cart before her, biting on it sometimes to ease the itching of her teething gums.

Valli's mother too lay on a charpoy in a far corner of the courtyard in the shade of the giant peepul tree. An unexpected winged guest, a bright blue *Neelkanth* had perched upon her shoulder and, without a care in the world, was dipping its black bill into the bowl of flattened rice and lentils Valli had placed for her.

"*Ram Naam Sat Hai...Ram Naam...*" A funeral procession, chanting the name of the true God Rama, passed outside their house.

The chanting must have drifted through the fog of her delirium; Anishta turned her head and glanced at Valli with eyes that seemed animated for a moment. Holding her burning, twisted fingers in his hand, he smiled down at her. Bending down, he whispered in her ear, "It's Marich."

He leaned back to observe the shadow of deep grief settling on her wretched face; tears slipped over the edge of her cheekbone and gathered in a tiny pool on the pillow. "I won't be long," he said rising, uncurling the fingers that had gridlocked around his hand trying to stay him.

Dust gathered like a thick film on everything that dotted the ugly Indian landscape: trees, leaves, cars, buildings, clothes, faces — anything that did not move for a minute gathered dust. Sweat glistened on the shiny black backs of tribal girls bent over lawns of guesthouses that lined the seashore, plucking dead grass and weed. Some of them squatted on the pavements in the shade of parked taxis while the drivers sprawled on the back seats, their feet sticking out the windows, old newspapers covering their faces from the salty, sticky wind.

The tide was coming in slowly now, and the wind had begun to work up a howl, which soon became a constant, loud shriek as it escaped over the mainland like a wild beast.

When Valli returned from the burning ghats, Anishta was no more.

SONAMARG —
SIX MONTHS EARLIER

"Why aren't you running?" the Captain barked, prodding the soldier doubled up in a shivering heap on the parapet lining the winding mountain road.

Sepoy Valli looked up, his face contorted in pain. He was bathed in sweat even though it was a bracing foggy morning. He clutched his stomach and groaned. "I can't," he managed to mumble through clenched teeth, slight foam gathering at the corner of his mouth.

"What's wrong with him?" the Captain spat at the Company Sergeant Major, while still prodding the soldier in his ribs with his thick baton.

"He's unwell, Sahib," the CSM replied deferentially.

"So? So what?"

"*Sahib*," the CSM said, lowering his voice, "people say he's possessed."

"Possessed! What a lame excuse! Even a fly cannot wander into this company line without permission. Sound a couple of chilly canes off his buttocks. He'll come to his senses."

"Sahib, whenever he goes on leave, he gets this problem. He's a fine runner otherwise."

"Don't send him on any leave then. Take him away and sort him out."

The CSM motioned at two men, who, without further ceremony, lifted Sepoy Valli between them and hauled him over the tailboard of a parked truck.

Later, after the morning parades and roll calls, the CSM marched into the barracks where Valli laid on a nylon charpoy, squirming in a fetal position, his head between his knees.

"What happens to you when you go on leave?" The CSM stood over Valli, tapping his cane on the steel frame of the charpoy.

"I don't know —" Valli turned to face him and managed to raise himself on an elbow. "Look —" he said, opening his mouth wide and sticking his black tongue out. Little worms crawled out his mouth, spreading over his face and neck, entering his nostrils and ears. They streamed down the bedposts and toward the CSM's shiny black boots. The CSM stepped back and stomped the slimy stains with his hobnailed boots, cursing all the while. Valli suddenly had a loud hiccup; his breath seemed caught up deep in his stomach, when he coughed out with great force a squirming inky ball the last trail of worms from his mouth. He collapsed back in his bed, exhausted, out like a wet light.

The CSM retreated from the barrack and stepped out into the grey mist that was settling like a heavy blanket over the mountain face. The damp stood thick on the tall green grass, the short day was spent already. He removed his beret, slung it on a tree branch, and wiped the sweat on his forehead. "*Oof*, what's up with him?" he asked, standing under the shade and lighting up a filterless cigarette. "Bad oral hygiene."

The Orderly NCO in charge of Valli's platoon shuffled his feet, tracing lines in the ground. "He screams all night, and he shits blood. Men don't want to use the latrines. He's wetting his bed and jabbers away to himself all the while."

"He looks shriveled."

"Hasn't touched a morsel since he came from home."

"Is it drink?"

"Hasn't touched a drop. We don't issue rum here at the post."

"Don't give him duty with a weapon. He'll shoot himself."

"He's a fine boy otherwise, does whatever you tell without grumbling. Pretty grounded, humble fellow."

"Folks?"

"Decent, poor people. Dad retired a respected postmaster. Stay by the sea in Odisha."

"Married?"

"Yeah, recently. Child marriage, I figure. Brought the bride home only last year. Young, very young. Got a small daughter too."

"Happens only when he goes home?"

"Yeah. Gets okay with time, though; recovers in the unit. But it's been getting worse each time. Do you think we should report him. The men understand, but for how long can they tolerate him?"

"The officers won't understand. They don't accept these things — things that can happen in rural areas. They'll say it's superstition."

"Maybe the doctors can help him?"

"They'll put him away in an isolation ward and give him shocks. He'll go nuts. Then we'll not only have a ghost, but a crazy ghost up our arse. And you know the manual. I'll have to put an armed guard on him, throw more good men after one problem case."

"What should I do with him?"

"Put him away on *Mandir* duties, let him help out *Panditji* for a few days. Then we'll see. Keep a keen eye on him." The CSM dropped the cigarette butt and ground it under his heel. "And make sure he brushes twice daily."

It was dark when Valli set down his trunk on the train platform. He looked around. There was nobody familiar. He looked in the crowd for the glowing face of his bride or the glazed eyes of his father that sparkled behind horn-rimmed glasses when they saw him, but they weren't there. He found an empty bench and waited.

The unmistakable smell of the sea mingled with fish and paddy fields wafted to his nostrils; smilingly, he inhaled deep gulps of it. It was humid, and he could taste the salt as he licked his lips. Just a few minutes on the station and little beads of moisture had sprung up on his arms already. His coarse uniform clung to him like sackcloth, and his neck began to itch where the collar touched it. There weren't many trains to Balasore at this hour, and the station began to empty out fast till it was just him, a few scruffy scavenger children, and stray curs that followed them on the feces- and urine-splattered train tracks. Suddenly becoming conscious of the overpowering stench around him, he rose and left.

He hailed down a cramped three-wheeler, noisy as a jackhammer, for an unmitigated ride that often excused minor grievances such as hearing loss and spinal trauma. The narrow, pot-holed road took them past the police colony, the district courts, the ramshackle shops selling expired medicines and bottled water to Bengali tourists on *Pooja* holidays, past the scarred remnants of the evening fish market, and finally past the vast submerged paddy fields and fish ponds that spawned toward the *Brahmani* backwaters draining into the Bay of Bengal. They soon cleared Balasore and were now speeding through the blue-black, overcast countryside of Chandipore, lit up by shimmering streaks on the Brahmani that caught the faint moonlight as it emptied into the sea.

Valli was annoyed. He expected to be welcomed at the station. Hadn't he written home of his arrival? But moping soon gave way to misgiving as a hundred negative thoughts crossed his mind. *Was his father well? Was the child sick? What if his wife was visiting her parents?* One could never be sure of the cadaverous Postman deciding not to visit your home. *But Valli had given him two bottles of army rum the last time, hadn't he?*

He therefore didn't bother to haggle with the driver as he dismounted at the rusty gates of his house. He banged the iron latch a couple of times to announce his arrival and entered.

Valli passed through the courtyard and entered the living room. His father was watching TV, and his daughter was playing at his knee. The old man, a heap of bones in a dirty dhoti, rose with delight on seeing his son. They hugged warmly, the daughter pressed between them.

"What's happening here, *Nana*?" Valli asked, looking around the untidy house. "Is Anishta taking care of you?" He stepped back and looked keenly at his father. The old man nodded his head and waved his frail hands in protest, or helplessness, saying nothing. "Where's *Bou*?"

Nana nodded toward a small partition in the wall covered by a frayed green curtain. Valli flicked the drape aside and entered the dimly lit room. His mother, propped up with pillows, lay on the bed. Covered with a hand-woven *Ikat* bed sheet, under which her face and long feet stuck out. She'd become so skinny, it was as if there was nothing underneath the sheet.

He took her hand and caressed it gently. She opened her eyes and squinted at him. "It's me, Bou. Valli. How are you?" he said and then had to repeat it louder close to her ear. The good half of her face crinkled into a smile, and she pulled him close. He hugged her, and they remained like that for a while, silently nuzzling against each other. "I've got you things, nice stuff to wear if you promise to get up from this bed. Okay?"

Bou nodded happily; she warbled and grunted but could say nothing. The sudden stroke had benumbed her limbs and speech. "Have you eaten?" he asked. "I'll be with Nana. You rest now. I'll see you in the morning. I'll take your bed out under the peepul, and you can feel the sea winds on your face and listen to the birds." He gently patted her head, straightened up, and left her.

"You have soda, Nana?" Valli opened the fridge; it was empty save a couple of water bottles, a plate of brown rice, and some fish cooked in mustard curry. "Where's the milk for the girl? Where's Anishta? Have you sent her out to the grocer for it?" He removed a water bottle and sank in the armchair next to Nana. Nana was absorbed in the TV and had turned up the volume as Valli was speaking.

"See what we have here," Valli said loudly, removing a bottle of Old Monk from his trunk and placing it with a flourish on the table. The old man's face lit up; he lowered the TV volume but couldn't still take his eyes off it. Valli poured out two stiff drinks, filled them up with water, and handed one to his father. "Cheers! Can we switch off the TV now, Nana? Where's Anishta?" Valli bent forward and took the baby off Nana's hands. She snuggled against his chest and was soon snoring softly.

"She'll be back soon. Why, it's quite dark already," Nana said, squinting out the window.

"Why's the house so dirty? Where's the food for the baby? Do you get the money orders I send?"

"Yes, yes — that *chodipua* postman — making eyes at womenfolk." Nana shook his head, knocking back the drink. "I get your letters, but I rarely go out now. Anishta manages everything. She's a good girl. Just look around you. That poor single bone has to take care of so much — and the fields. She's gone to get *Illish* for you. Don't get angry with her. Have you seen the crops? The castor stands so tall and proud, ripe for harvest."

"What about your pension? Aren't you keeping a maid," he remarked, looking around the untidy house.

"Anishta says we can't afford one anymore. Insists on doing all the work herself. Won't let anyone enter the house."

"Why? Why weren't you there at the station? Why couldn't she come? I've come after so long. They wouldn't give me leave after the way I fell ill the last time."

"Where would I leave your mother? Who would take care of the baby?"

"Still." Valli's scowled.

"How do you feel now, *Pua*," the old man asked, patting his son's hand.

"I feel better in the unit. I've lived here all my life. I love the sea, and now it seems this weather doesn't suit me — or any of us."

"Well, take care this time. Let's drink to us," Nana said, holding up his empty glass. They drank steadily, laughing and talking of good old days when coconut water was still cheap, when Bou haggled with Bangladeshi refugees who came on their rickety little canoes and sold pomfrets and prawns on the beach, and when the guns still boomed from the naval firing ranges nearby.

A hush fell on the house when they heard laughing voices outside, the tinkle of glass bangles, and the chime of silver anklets on slim, pirouetting ankles. Valli unconsciously ran his fingers through his hair and straightened up in the chair. The curtains parted, and a dusky, enchanting face peeped in. Anishta, light on her feet, bounded over the hearth and shyly covered her head with the edge of her sari. She touched the feet of both men and stood giggling against the wall, casting coy glances at her husband. She seemed the only one in this house in fine clothes and looking filled out. The weather agreed with her, at least.

"*Kemoti achho tumi*, eh," Valli asked after her, his anger all gone at her loveliness. Anishta bit the edge of her sari, swayed like a child, and giggled some more. "Who was with you? Whom were you talking to?"

The girl froze. "Nobody," she said. "Some passing fisherwomen."

"Good. You've made friends?" Valli rose and took the bulging jute shopping bag from her. He peeped in it. "What did you get?"

"Illish," she replied. "Pumpkin and gourd for *pitamata*."

Valli helped her empty the contents of her shopping on the kitchen counter. "What are these," he asked, finding vials and wrappers.

"Medicines."

"But there are no markings. Aren't they supposed to be tablets? Where's the prescription slip?"

"He doesn't give," she said, cowering, afraid he'll strike her.

"You're going to some local quack, aren't you? Why don't you go to the army doctor in Balasore?"

"Alone? It's too far." She trembled. Her round eyes became wide with fear, and she turned her face protectively.

Valli threw up his arms in frustration. "Your parents should have lettered you. You can't even find your way around town. How are you going to teach our child? It's all my fault. I'll get them the medicines, enough to last a few months." He gripped her arms and glowered down at her. Her sari fell off her shoulders revealing bony collarbones on which one could balance an egg, he thought, and a heaving bosom. Pushing her against the wall, Valli pulled down her blouse and planted his lips on her bare breasts, slurping loudly. Her skin tone was much lighter under her clothes where the harsh sun had not cast his burning gaze. She sucked in her breath as his moustache bristled against her baby skin. He released her when he heard his father shuffling about in the other room.

"You are not to visit a quack again, understand?"

She nodded eagerly, relieved to be spared a boxing on the ears.

He cupped her oval face in his hands and looked deep into her hazel eyes. "After dinner then…" he leaned close and whispered, his hot rummy breath lingering as he left her to cook the fish.

Anishta smoked the Illish in young plantain leaves and prepared it with mustard seed paste, curd, and eggplant, before submitting it to the frying pan for the final assault.

"It's a work of art," Valli said, wiping his mouth at the edge of her sari even as his father burped loudly to show appreciation for the dish served well. Valli finished off his plate before his father did. As he was about to lean forward and pick a piece from his father's plate, Anishta slapped him playfully on the wrist. "Have patience, *upapati*. I'll get you a separate plate," she said, rushing into the kitchen.

"Why can't I eat from my father's Illish?"

"I spice it lightly for him. You'll lose the taste. Wait up."

Later, after Valli had put the parents and child to bed, he led Anishta by the hand to the roof where they used to sleep in the cooler sea breeze of the night. The winds had died down with the receding tide, and the palms gently brushed across the half moon that seemed to hang at the edge of the terrace. They could see the little lights of fishing trawlers out at the sea peering through the lifting clouds. They sat awhile on the jute charpoy, holding hands, gazing out at the beautiful gloomy expanse of the Indian Ocean before them. Little hillocks rose out of the black emptiness that stretched out as far as the eye could see and then merged into the dark rumbling skies. Valli sighed in peace. He was home. No artist could imitate God in the beautiful things that He had created on this planet, Valli mused.

"Sing a song," Anishta said, curling up on her side, placing her head in his lap.

"All right," he said. Clearing his throat, he began:

"The river runs black, then red;
By soldiers' hands my child's bled.
I have dark breasts, black thighs,
And a shadowy belly under even blacker skies:
My child weeps, and hungry it sleeps."

"Who do you mean?" Anishta asked.

"It's just a song, silly bird," he said. Bending down, he kissed her on the lips. Lifting her, he unwound her sari around her boyish hips and cupped her cool buttocks. He pushed up her blouse and began to suck at her upturned nipples. "Are you still suckling the girl?" he laughed, detaching his face and wiping his lips. She grabbed his hair and pulled him back to her bosom, moaning softly. He rubbed his mouth on her moist breasts and drank of her some more. Suddenly he pulled back and spat on the ground. He wiped his mouth with the back of his hand and held out his arm against the moonlight. Standing up, he cursed, "*Fusa chata!*" as he grabbed her shoulders and turned her to face the moon. Her chest was covered in blood. "What is it?" he screamed.

Anishta first looked down at her naked body and then tilted her head toward the moon and laughed as if she were mocking its cleverness. "You bit me, lover," she said.

"No, I didn't. I swear."

"Yes you did." She lifted her sari from the ground and quickly gathering it about her naked body and bounded down the rickety spiral wooden staircase to their bedroom where the child lay.

Valli followed her down and then drew water with an aluminum ladle from an earthen pot placed by the bed and washed himself. He fell back on the bed, and sat there worrying, his head in his hands.

He felt hung over when he awoke in the morning. The night before was hazy in his numb mind. He thought a head massage might do him some good, so he sent for the village barber. The *nayee* was chatty as usual, full of gossip about who was beating his wife and who was drinking too much rice beer in the village.

"I need to see the postmaster about Nana's pension and my money orders, so give me a nice grooming today," Valli told him, when he managed to get a word in between the nayee's nonstop patter.

"Why, any problems?" the nayee asked, his interest perked up; he examined Valli's head to see how he might shorten already crew-cut hair. Slashing his scissors against the comb with aplomb, he went snip-snip on Valli's head anyway.

"I think they might be shortchanging Anishta. She can't read, you know. I want to know what happens to all the money sent home. Nana will never complain."

"It's great to have money, greater to spend it."

"Provided you have it to spend."

"Wasn't your father postmaster himself? They won't stop from robbing their own, is it?"

"People who knew him are long gone."

"It's a bad deal to be a soldier. They're away so long. You never know what fish is frying behind your back. It's fishy, but," the nayee said, snorting.

"What do you mean?"

"How much time do you have this leave?"

"Two months."

"That's good for you, then. Your wife won't be lonely."

"She's got my parents and the baby. Why would she be lonely?" Valli sniggered.

"Yeah, why would *she* be lonely?" And then lowering his voice, the barber said, "She has visitors enough from her old village."

"I'm glad," Valli said curtly, shutting the door firmly on the barber's intrusion into his family affairs for gossip.

"Would *he* be glad, indeed? There's a time to plant and a time to uproot. A time to keep and a time to throw away."

"You speak in riddles, man." Valli began to turn his head, but the nayee firmly tipped his chin forward with the handle of his knife.

"Don't speak, or you'll be hurt. A time to speak and a time to be silent," he said.

Before a confused Valli could quip and repartee, Anishta's clear voice rang out from the courtyard below. "Aayi, *aapono* come down and have some tea and sweet meats…and bring along the nayee also."

"There, you're done," said the barber, tilting Valli's chin, and examining his handiwork. "Smooth like a girl."

"Let's go," Valli said, flinging off the sheet. "Refreshments await us. You haven't heard of Anishta's *chhena jalebis*, have you?"

"There isn't much I haven't heard about her," the barber smirked. "But first, I must clean up the floor."

"Do it afterward." Valli grasped his arm and nudged him ahead down the creaking staircase.

Anishta had drawn out a charpoy and placed it in the shade of the old peepul. Two bell metal plates with steaming hot deep-fried flatbreads and dry peas gravy, red hued from the chillies, had been laid out. A large copper bowl of hot jalebis, covered with a newspaper to keep away the flies, sat by for sweet relief in case the mouth caught fire.

Nana sat cross-legged at one edge of the cot, adjusting his glasses on his nose so that he could eye the repast better. "Come, come," he waved them onward, impatient to begin.

The three men squatted on the narrow cot and began to apply themselves vigorously to the nourishment, licking their fingers as well as whiskers. Anishta sprinted to and fro from the kitchen, barely managing to keep the bowls full. At long last when they were done, the men slurped masala chai from earthen cups loudly, rubbing their hands over their bellies, and talked of the rising price of land and of bathing in the holy river.

The skies overcast and the sea breeze salty and sticky on their lips, the ruddy shelduck honking overhead and the frogs croaking below, the rain a-coming, and not else to be done this day, the men dozed for a bit in the cool shade.

Faint rumblings in the distant sea brought the men out of their pleasant afternoon siesta. "I must clean the roof before it rains," the barber announced again, swinging his skinny dhoti-clad brown legs over the cot.

"Anishta will do it," Valli said, stretching, deeply inhaling of the far-off rain in the breeze.

"Never leave these things to someone else. I keep a clean shop, sir," the barber retorted and clambered up the stairs. Soon after he looked over the parapet, puzzled, and shouted to the somnambulant men below. "Hey, what happened to the shavings and the nail clippings? Have you seen them?"

The two men looked at each other and shook their heads. Nana turned over his side and went back to sleep.

"Strange." The barber came back to the wall after some more searching and fretting.

"Anishta must have swept the floor, *Kakei*. Come down," Valli said.

The barber wasn't satisfied. He looked around some more and then came down grumbling.

Meanwhile, hearing the men awake and talking, Anishta had also come out, the baby suckling at her half-covered breast, its tiny hands clawing her face. "The wind might have blown them away. Why make a fuss?" she said.

"So you didn't sweep the roof?" Valli said.

"No, not every day," she replied.

"The wind is too light. The floor has been swept clean," the nayee said, eyeing them suspiciously.

"So what? It's just garbage done with," Valli said.

"So what? In the wrong hands, mischief can be done. I should have cleaned the floor then," the nayee went out, muttering to himself.

"What's his problem, weird old man," Valli asked. Playfully biting Anishta's free breast over the blouse and guffawing when she howled in pain.

The blood-star ascends against a bleak sky,
Whose dome shrouds the orange sun
Setting in the blue-black sea,
Foaming, when it meets the white sand:
Beware, the false flatteries of dawn.

Valli sang moodily when he returned from the post office. He rummaged through the almirah to get the passbooks. He became increasingly anxious as he compared them with the post office statements he'd got from the postmaster. Anishta, sensing him troubled, fussed over him, quiet like a mouse. But he kicked away the stool on which she'd placed tea and vegetable pancakes when he saw his face had been cut out from their joint photograph in one of the books.

"Where's my photo gone?" he shouted.

"I...I u-u-used it to apply for the g-gas connection. I didn't have a ph-photo of yours in the house."

He stomped on the fallen dishes with rising rage and screamed above the clatter: "You said you were unlettered!"

"I am," she whispered, her eyes wide.

"Then how come you signed on the post office receipts instead of your thumb impression?"

"Nana taught me how to write my name. That's all I know."

"Nana! Where's he? And who's this young lout who accompanies you?"

"No one."

"The postmaster told me. Com'on; tell me!" he crushed her slender wrist in his grip and pulled her down on her knees beside him. He yanked her hair bun till her brows pulled all the way to the end of her forehead.

"It's…it's Marich…my…my cousin brother from my village."

"A cousin. Where the hell was he all this while? Why does he come? Com'on. Speak up, slut!"

"The…the postmaster makes eyes at me. I'm afraid. And Nana doesn't walk that far nowadays. Marich…he comes on the first to walk with me to get Nana's pension and your money orders."

"The accounts are empty. The statements match perfectly. Everything has been credited. Then where's all the money gone? Who've you given it to?"

"I spent it on us. Ouch!" she cried as he gave one final pull and released her. She trembled like a leaf on a rock face; covering her face in her hands, as if she feared to be struck. A flood of tears broke out of her almond eyes and trickled through the dam of her small fingers.

"You've been sending money back home to your parents, haven't you?" he yelled.

She nodded and gripped his feet. "They're so poor and weak, Valli! Please, the castor failed again this season. The water is so salty."

Their daughter also began to cry in the other room. His arms hanging loosely by his sides, Valli gazed at his child-wife helplessly. He dropped the passbooks and pulled her to his knees. "Hush," he said soothingly, "there, there. No more, child. See, it's all right. You should've told me, shouldn't you've?'

She nodded and rested her petite head, thickly decked with wild tresses, on his strong thighs. They were like that for a long time. Later, when Nana came home — he was fond of squatting in the village square with his friends, smoking hookah — Valli brought out the Old Monk, and they started drinking.

Valli never again mentioned money to his Nana. The headache from the morning hadn't gone, and Valli began to feel a slight hotness rise in his flesh. He could barely peck at the mustard fish curry and rice Anishta had prepared only for him and fell asleep early, strangely exhausted for not doing any work.

By morning, a full-blown fever had taken charge of Valli. It grew worse, and over the next few days, Valli went into a delirium, tossing on the bed and hallucinating. His body burnt to the touch, as if on fire, without breaking into sweat. Nana and Anishta took turns sponging him with cold packs, day and night. Valli felt as if he had touched the devil himself. He threw up every liquid poor Anishta fed him from the soup bowl. He mumbled to himself and felt himself floating near the ceiling, from where he could look down at his body.

He felt disoriented, and his thoughts jostled him from one fragmented memory to another at breakneck speed. Scenes flickered from his life like a fast-forwarded, moth-eaten reel. He drifted in and out of consciousness. The sky became full of blue turtles and mammoth white crocodiles, and a little boy, who looked uncannily like himself, caught in the swirling wind and kept going round and round, calling out for help. His arm fell off, and he tried to snatch it from an ashen man in black robes, who was chewing on it, but he could not move an inch. His body was not obeying any commands. He wrenched himself with great effort from the long fingers that snaked around his broken body and tried to stay conscious, but they kept coming back, dragging him into the dark cesspools of his frenzied hallucinations.

But Valli fought hard and long, and the salve of modern medicine began to ease his anguished spirit. On the fourth day, he finally woke up, as Nana's voice seemed to drift over to him, as if in a dream.

"Where's Anishta," he asked, suddenly sitting up in his bed drenched cold with his sweat.

Nana shuffled over to him and held a glass of water to his mouth. Valli felt its coolness soothing his insides, which were dry as dust. "Rest now, son."

"No, where's she?" Valli asked hoarsely. "I must find her." He flung away the hand-woven linen sheet and rushed out barefoot in the dark; his father raised a feeble arm to stay him, but Valli, his eyes wild and his clothes askew, wouldn't be restrained.

In the gray haze, dull shafts of white streetlights shone off spinach-dark trees brooding against a melancholy orange of invisible sky, as Valli passed though the sleepy village. Little pebbles bit into his feet, but he charged on, madly along crisscrossing pathways through mustard and paddy fields. When he neared his farmstead, he saw a dull red light from the windows of the barn next to the tube well. Never before had his fields looked so well cared for. A luxurious blanket of yellow and gold mustard in bloom spread over his land. As he edged closer toward the barn, he could make out by the glow of its lamp an outline of two naked bodies entwined on a soft mound of fodder and mulch. He sank on his knees, suddenly unable to go any further. The lovers' whispers carried in the moist breeze over to him; he knew then that one was his unfaithful wife and the other the man she addressed as Marich, both cavorting vulgarly in the open, with all of nature as witness.

The couple untangled after a while and dressed. Then they took the path through the fields toward the river, Anishta following the other in her unmistakable, languorous, swaying gait that no wide-eyed man in the village could be saved from. His shame giving him strength, Valli struggled to his feet and began to follow them.

After an hour's plodding in the riverbank, which was increasingly turning marshy, the river narrowed, and the mangroves became close and dense, almost brushing their faces. Soon they could see white, salt-water crocodiles, lit up by the moon, lazing about in the swamps on the far bank.

Mosquitos bit Valli relentlessly, and the heat and humidity made his clothes stick to his body like another layer of skin. After a few hours, the path along the river turned into a small fork and the creek petered off into a shallow pool. The pair ahead rolled up their robes and tied them around their waist and waded across the swamp. Marich led the way. He seemed to glide on the swamp, rather than walk, taking the second step before the first one had completed, making sure both his feet were on the ground at the same time. Anishta hastened after him, carefully trailing his footprints by the glow of the silvery skies on the white swamp.

Valli could see the tracks made on the slippery sands by the swamp snakes and crocs and fervently prayed not to run into them. The small party soon entered the thick mangroves that grow very closely together. Marich had grabbed Anishta's hand and was steering her on the cattails and reeds that supported them on the marsh.

Before midnight, they had crossed over the swamp and reached a firm mud flat surrounded by a spotless pond. A small hut sat in the middle of the ground, a flickering light and curling smoke coming from within it. A loud shout by Marich brought a burning lantern to the door, held by a young boy in black robes. The hut was low, maybe about five feet high. The boy bent and came out toward them. He and Marich exchanged a few words, and the boy went back in.

Valli crept forward on his haunches and hid himself in a small bush close by from where he could observe and overhear those gathered about the hut. The boy returned shortly and spread a small rug outside the hut and set the lantern by it. A tall, skinny *Aghori*, a tantric, soon came out of the hut and greeted the couple by raising his hand in blessings. The couple touched the ground at his feet and took out two bottles of Old Monk — Valli's army-issue rum — a packet of *ganja*, nice marijuana, some hair — Valli's hair — wrapped in a newspaper, and a thick wad of notes — Valli's money — from a sling bag and placed them before him. The Aghori seemed pleased and blessed them again. The party squatted on the rug next to him.

The Aghori was a bearded, skinny sadhu smeared in ash from a funeral pyre. He wore two red dots and a black square mark on his forehead. His chest was covered in vermilion, and he wore a white loincloth with four knots. He had loosely tied his matted locks on top of his head, over which sat a wobbly black turban. The urchin placed a human skull filed off to a saucer's shape before the *sadhu* and two steel glasses before the other men. The urchin poured out the local liquor for them, while the sadhu pulled out a chillum and greedily filled it with ganja.

The men smoked and drank awhile, the Aghori often asking Anishta questions about Valli and his life in the army.

"*Swamiji*, when will the work be done?" Marich folded his hands and asked finally. "Other than a general sickness, from which both seem to come out after some time, there's nothing happening. They are still alive."

"Only when we are prepared to give up everything," the Aghori replied, "are the gods willing to grant us our wishes; I am confident, with time you will succeed. I see you have brought what I sought," he said, poking with the end of his chillum the contents of the newspaper wrapper in which Anishta had neatly bundled Valli's hair, nails, and a small cutout photograph.

"When will the end come? Our daughter is growing. We want to return with her to our village," Marich asked in an ingratiating tone.

"Nothing is hidden from a true tantric, son. I can snatch a person from the blackest pits of *Patal Lok*. Let us waste no further time, we are already past midnight, and we have only until 2 a.m. I will now perform the *shava-asana*. He barked to the urchin to bring him a fresh corpse. "You help him," he ordered Marich.

The urchin and Marich set off in the direction of the marshes across the pond. Many local tribals still preferred to immerse their dead in the holy Brahmani River, rather than cremate them in the Hindu way at the burning *ghats* upstream. Where the river forked, some corpses got wedged in the marshes and the mangrove roots. The marshes swallowed them and threw them up again after several days.

The bodies got washed away in fresh currents, but more got lodged again, giving an endless and ready supply for the tantric's practice, as well as his food. For, the tantrics are cannibals, and eating excreta and burning human flesh at the pyre or from the floating carcasses is gold-standard behavior. They feel an uncontrollable urge for human flesh and will eat it raw if hungry. This Aghori claimed he could eat an entire body dragged from the pyre, if he chose to. The more they blur the lines between right and wrong, holy and the unholy, clean and the unclean, the closer they edge toward self-realization as a true tantric believer.

While the men were gone, the Aghori pushed Anishta down on the ground and forced himself upon her. She struggled meekly under him, but soon caved in to his promises, as well as threats to harm her lover and daughter. Valli felt the fever take control of him completely, and he could but helplessly watch, his limbs not answering to him at all.

The scene before him sickly evoked in his frenzied mind the first time he himself had known her body. They had been married off, as per custom, when she was only a child. She'd stayed back with her folks till she attained puberty, and then Valli's parents brought her home with great ceremony. Seven un-widowed women had applied turmeric paste on her body and made her wear a tilak, a holy mark on the forehead, with rice, before he could consummate his union with her. Afterward, they had eaten together from a roasted coconut, and she'd offered him saffron milk on the first night.

She must have met Marich when she was growing up in her village, Valli told himself. *Now she wants her husband and his father out of the way, obviously. Is it her mind working, or Marich's? He seems a handsome rascal. Anyway, how did it matter – she was still conspiring with him, wasn't she?*

He began to sing softly, under his breath, to himself mostly:
"This maddening twilight that spreads
Like a pall on the quivering deep,
Comes from the land where my sweetheart lives.
She is the maid with tresses dressed with sweet-smelling blooms;
Fear and shyness are her weapons whilst she crisscrosses the earth hunting for game.
Men are the unsuspecting game caught in the beauty trap of this false woman,
The words of the fish-eyed damsel are now meaningless to me."

By the time the men returned, dragging a corpse by the legs, the Aghori was done with Anishta. Anishta had washed herself at the pond and readjusted her sari, while the Aghori had filled his chillum afresh and was singing to himself without a care in the world:
"This is empty,
That is empty,

Emptiness sets forth from emptiness.
If you take away the emptiness, it is still empty."

The men dragged the corpse inside the hut. Stung by a morbid curiosity, Valli managed to crawl on all fours and reach the low-slung window from where he could peer inside hunched on his knees. On the way, he'd grabbed Marich's still-burning chillum and inhaled deeply from it, which instantly numbed his pain and lifted the haze in his head.

The hut was brightly lit with kerosene lanterns and choking with heavy incense smoke. Fierce flames spat out of a fire burning in a crack in the baked mud floor, stoked by the urchin splashing *desi* liquor into it for spectacular effects. A mound of brown rice was placed by the fire, painted with red and black stripes at its base, and embedded with limes, fruits, bones, and other strange objects. A wooden stake was buried in the floor, with long white hair tied to it.

The corpse was placed in a corner on the floor, and the Aghori sat on its groin facing the head, chanting his mantras. The others crouched around the fire, fascinated. The urchin tossed into the fire a gooey mixture from a bowl in rhythm with the chants. The bowl looked like it contained a mixture made from standard ingredients: oil, human excreta, and flesh. They passed on the bowl to the party asking them to make offerings into the fire.

The Aghori placed a skull on the corpse's head and an *Atma Ram* on top of it.

This is a small bone, nearly a perfect model of a person, called Atma Ram – having arms, legs, head, and other parts of the body, resembling a saint in *Samadhi* or deep trance. In a good person, it is found undiminished, full. It is believed that the *suksham shareer* (essence) or the *jeev atma* (soul) lives in this bone. This *param atma* (eternal soul) lives in between our two eyes, in the form of the light of millions of suns but very cool and pleasant. Knowledgeable Hindu relatives insist on seeking the Atma Ram when they collect the *flowers* — or the remaining bones in the cooling pyre on the fourth day after cremation, for immersion in the holy Ganges. Said to contain the soul of the departed person, tantrics steal it from burning pyres soon after the cremation process. They use it to invoke the immaterial spirits for their practice.

The Aghori was now chanting hysterically, rocking to and fro, and the urchin was lobbing the mixture and liquor into the fire in livid frenzy. Suddenly the Aghori stopped. He drew a sharp knife and severed off the corpse's arm. He started gnawing on the arm, snarling and gulping down the flesh. After chewing some, he threw the arm at the urchin, who placed it in a tin pot filled with water and set it on the fire for boiling.

The Aghori grabbed the liquor bottle and took long swigs from it like a terribly thirsty man. He swung his legs off the corpse and dragged deeply from his chillum, exhausted by the *asana*.

He reached into a small trunk and tipped some green and black powder separately into newspaper pieces, which he folded expertly. He also poured out the contents of the bowl into a small brown glass bottle and handed everything over to Anishta. "The black mixture is stronger, for Valli, and the other for his father. Your job should be done under a week. If not, next you'll have to bring me either his semen, or blood, and then I will chant the final mantra, which can be very dangerous for all of us — but I don't think that will be necessary. No one has resisted the power of the shava asana, the mantra that I have cast on your husband and father-in-law today. That is all now, my children – the dawn arrives, I shall rest now. Leave in peace — may you have many offspring," he said, motioning them to leave.

Marich nudged Anishta, and after touching the Aghori's feet, they left by the same way through the swamp and the fields beyond.

Valli — buoyed by the marijuana, leaned against the hut, and waited for dawn before he knocked on that hut's door. He was tired, hungry, and covered in filth, but his head and spirit were quite spotless and lucid now.

There was no need for Anishta to burn like this; no need, for the candle of life of one so young and beautiful, to be snuffed out like this. And there was definitely no need, for Valli to be lighting up his child bride's funeral pyre, like this.

The holy Brahmani, placid, and on course to be swallowed by the ocean, lapped at his unshod feet. But Valli felt he was being tossed around in a tiny boat without a life vest – in a black raging storm with crackling thunder and hammering deluge. The incessant wail of mantras on the Burning Ghats didn't ring; it vibrated, like a cosmic howl, churning up grief and ache. The stench of burning corpses swirled around him, and he could feel the heat of their dying embers cooking the eyeballs inside the skulls. It was as if he, himself, had been struck a crumbling blow of the undertaker's staff, dispatching his soul on its next flight to another mortal abode.

"Strange for one to die so young, and so suddenly," the grieving village women, beating their breasts as per custom, wailed.

"Oh, what will become of her daughter?"

"What will be Nana's fate — even his wife has deserted him for her heavenly abode."

BALASORE RAILWAY STATION
— THE DEPARTURE

Soon after the funeral, Valli had packed up a few of their meager belongings and reserved train berths for Jabalpur, where his unit had moved after the field tenure. The Captain had accepted Valli's request for priority allotment of family accommodation on extreme compassionate grounds, considering there was no one to look after the child and his ailing father now.

"I am a burden on you, son," Nana bemoaned, as they sat on the platform at Balasore. "You should have left me to live out my last days in the village. How will you take care of the baby alone — you should have remarried, and left your brood at home."

"Never again," Valli said.

"But you'll be lonely, without Anishta, without a wife."

"I see Anishta in her — don't you think so, Nana?" Valli said, holding up the baby, who looked far better now, smiling to herself in her sleep.

Nana nodded, but remained quiet. Perhaps he knew. The daughter hadn't taken after Valli's features at all.

"We must give this girl the best," Valli said, holding his father's gaze. "Won't we?"

Nana took the baby from him and hugged her close. "Yes, my son," he said, his eyes moist. "Isn't it strange," he said after a pause, "that we should recover, and Anishta should fall ill — as if she'd reaped our maladies?"

"She reaped as she'd sowed, Nana. Perhaps she wanted everything of ours — so she got it. There's nothing strange."

"But there are strange mischiefs afoot — unwholesome murmurs. Of a powerful tantric being around in these parts…sudden deaths…

fields struck down by pests…water wells souring over…business ruin. He lives in the swamp by the river — you know of it?"

"He's nothing more than a businessman with strange powers, Nana. So, it's not hard to persuade such a man, with incentives, to reverse his magic, and prescribe it on the very person who practices it. You can say, Nana, a taste of your own medicine."

〤〤〤 〤〤〤 〤〤〤 〤

About the Author

Nidhi Singh lives with her husband in the mountains close to McLeodganj (the abode of the Dalai Lama). She attended American International School, Kabul, before moving to Delhi University for her bachelor's of arts in English Honors. Her short work has been published by Digital Fiction Publishing Co, LA Review of LA, *Flame Tree Publishing, Firefly Magazine, Four Ties Lit Review, The Insignia Series*, Inwood Indiana Press, Bards and Sages Publishing, *So To Speak, Scarlet Leaf Review, Bewildering Stories, Down in the Dirt, Mulberry Fork Review,* tNY.Press, *Fabula Argentea, Aerogram, Asvamegha,* Flash Fiction Press and elsewhere. Her translations of Sikh Holy Scriptures, essays on Bollywood, and a few novels are available in print and online.

POPPY LANE

Dana Himrich

My bones rattle me awake. When I open my eyes, I can see the whole room trembling. The stones of the farmhouse wall shake within the confines of their mortar, the old wooden shelves scream and creak, and Grandmère's little old watercolor has broken from its nail and fallen to the floor once again. Through the hole in the rotting shingles, a dark and immense shape is moving through the gray clouds.

An airship! Scrambling out of bed and not bothering to lace my boots as I pulled them on, I run to the window and open the frayed curtains. The panes of glass which the frame once held are long gone, letting me climb onto the sill and dangle my legs over the edge.

I've seen so many airships, good and bad, yet I still don't know what I ought to think. The doughboys who have gone up in them say it is a wonderful feeling. I wonder if it is the same in the bad ones. The ones that fly so high you can hardly see them, which haven't come bringing aid to the soldiers and country folk. The ones that gave London and Paris fire in exchange for bullets that did nothing.

This ship is bad: you can tell straight away. It is painted all in black but for the Kaiser's golden eagle on its side. Four propellers as big as a house on each side and yet another in the back…must be a new model. On its underside, they have printed the year of deployment in dark red. 1929, this year. Fifteenth year of the Great War.

"Alfred!" a voice behind me hisses a moment before its owner pulls me back inside. "Stay down; they'll see you."

I wrench myself free and stick out my tongue. "We've nothing they would want. And you're too ugly to be one of their wives."

Emilie is nearly a lady, nine years older than me. She might still find a nice young man to court her, Grandmère says, if there are any still alive. Soldiers don't count, for they're dead men from the moment they enlist. So, my sister's skin has gone ruddy from work, and she bartered her hair to keep us in firewood. What has grown back looks more like straw, and she holds it from her face in a stubby little braid.

"You know it isn't about what they want," she hisses at me as she closes the curtains. "What would the townsfolk do for crops if our earth was scoured?"

"They've plenty of earth already," I answer, shrugging. "I don't care if it's a bad ship or not. It's still the only fun I have around here."

Emilie puts a finger to her lips and shakes her head. "You mustn't say such things around Grandmère."

Suddenly, we hear a great clatter from downstairs, and an even greater shriek. Emilie gasps as she hurries down the ladder to the first floor of the farmhouse, and I scramble after her.

Grandmère is sitting in her rocking chair by the window, shaking like she has seen Grandpère's ghost. In her hands is our only lamp, which she grips as she stares up at the ceiling. The little table beside her has been knocked on its side in her haste. When Emilie touches her arm, she is nearly struck.

"No, no," Emilie whispers, gently patting Grandmère's arm. "It's only us. Emilie and Alfred. No Germans here."

The fire in Grandmère's clouded eyes begins to die, and her grip on the lamp loosens enough for us to take it away. For a few moments, she sits quietly, her hands folded in her lap as though she is ashamed. Then she whispers, "There are always Germans here."

Grandmère and Emilie can remember the beginning of the war, that warm day six years before I came along when someone shot the archduke. "Back then, they all said it was only for fun," Grandmère tells us. "Something to keep us busy until Noël." And then she spits.

Grandpère rotted in a trench back when the fighting was still in this corner of France, and Papa's biplane went down over the Channel before I was born. Grandmère took Emilie and Mama in, thinking they would only stay until I was born. But Mama lost too much blood that night, and even Grandmère could not turn away a newborn and a girl in the dead of winter. So, when morning came, she made Emilie help her dig Mama's grave.

No, Grandmère is not a kind woman. She would not have lived this long if she was. Nor is she cruel, not without cause. "To survive," she often says, "you must be of use to someone."

The people in town need supplies: food, weapons, medicine, news from loved ones in the west. The soldiers who pass by on their way to the front lines need a distraction. No one is better than Grandmère at making things go where they are needed. When our field and garden are ripe, and our animals have given all they can, she takes what she can carry and goes into town. Those who have nothing can take what they need, but those with wares to trade must barter with Grandmère. They fix our broken tools, give her seeds or an animal somewhat less sickly. The priest always seems to have a spare bottle of communion wine in the cellar. Soldiers pay well for a glass or three when they stumble across the farmhouse. They do not ask where it comes from — or why their guns and kits are a little emptier when they wake.

Grandmère presents us with her newest haul as we scrape the last spoonfuls of water-clogged porridge from our bowls. Four boxes of bullets, a bottle of laudanum, and a small cloth pouch that she opens. Twenty German coins spill on to the tabletop. Our eyes gleam at the clattering pieces of metal, worthless as they are.

"The bottle must go to Madame Thierry," Grandmère mumbles as though trying to remind herself. "The rest goes to the church." There is already a basket of cans and vegetables sitting next to the front door. "Be back by midday."

Emilie nods while looking down at the table. "Yes, Grandmère." She stands up like a machine and starts to clear the table.

"You must take the old path."

We both stop where we are and look up at her. "You mean it?" I ask, smiling. Emilie looks as pale as a sheet.

"*Oui.*"

Emilie's hands begin to shake. "But, Grandmère…"

She raps her cane on the floorboards. "Go."

"We will, Grandmère." Emilie finishes picking up the dishes and cleans them slowly, now frowning. "Alfred, get your coat."

The new path from our farm to the village is long and winds east, past the remains of the old battlefield. The old path is much quicker, and it passes right through what was once no man's land. When our men still held this part of France, that ground was full of barbed wire and the empty shells of bullets. Grandmère says you could hear the guns from miles and miles away. They buried the dead soldiers here when the war was just starting out, before everyone learned how the Treatment could make them useful again. Emilie says that is all nonsense, and there is nothing buried there but old land mines. She would know: she saw a boy step on one. She won't tell me what it looked like.

I run ahead of Emilie, searching for things that the soldiers from long ago have dropped. A dead man often loses his helmet, or someone passing through will leave behind his fine knife when he stops to rest, and these we can use. I also run because I know I can make Emilie take my shortcut if I reach the trench first.

We needed a new path to the village because the soldiers dug a trench across our old one. They hadn't any time to fill it in before they could flee, so it is there still after all these years, cutting across the bottom of the hill. It is ten feet long and just as deep, and it goes nearly to the edge of our village. Grandmère and Emilie don't like it, but it is quicker than either path.

I run down the hill and jump into the trench. We've just had a good rain, so the mud is soft again; I sink up to the tops of my boots in an instant.

"See what good that did you?" Emilie has stopped at the edge of the trench, her face red from running and yelling curses at my back.

"This is a better way to the village, Emilie."

"I'm taking the bridge."

"Then I will meet you on the other side!" I pull my legs out from the mud and begin to walk west, where the village lies. A moment later, Emilie lands at my side. "I'll beat you later if Grandmère doesn't."

Our men took nothing with them when they left this place. The wooden platforms and roads are still there, and so are the little caves they carved out of the walls to place their beds in. The mud is full of bags carrying old food or a deck of cards or a letter that crumbles when you try to read it. Piles of dirt and rocks fell across the path when the walls grew weak and collapsed; that is where you might find a helmet or a boot or pieces of bone. By now they are getting harder to see, because the grass and the poppies are growing over them.

This ground doesn't seem to want any flowers other than poppies. They grow everywhere there. We mostly find them just beyond the trench, but just as often they come out of old footprints or the cracks in the wall.

"Each one of them is a soul, you know," Grandmère once told us. "That is why there are so many in that place." In town, they call it Poppy Lane.

The far end of the trench is shallow. More men died here, the grown-ups say, because the walls fell down so often. There are certainly more of the dirt piles; Emilie and I have to walk on top of them to go on. Spots of green, red, and white catch my eyes. Stuck halfway in the dirt are a scuffed hat and a skull.

Emilie stops. "Do you think he was somebody important?"

"No one liked him if he was," I answer, pointing out the poppies growing from his eye sockets. I reach down to take the hat, but Emilie shoves my hand away.

"Don't touch it!" she says.

"Why not? He doesn't need it anymore. Besides, it'll sell for something in town. Grandmère takes things from the soldiers all the time."

"Never from the dead ones."

"But they aren't around to care!"

Emilie must have been hoping for more than that, because she frowns and shakes her head. "Keep walking toward town," she says, handing me her basket of goods. "I'll follow you later."

"What are you stopping for?"

"I said *go,* Alfred."

She is in the sort of state where she never answers my questions, so I stick my tongue out at her and begin walking again. Emilie stays where she is, watching as though I must be gone before she can do whatever she stopped to do. When I am far enough away from her, I duck behind a pile of rocks and peer back at her. She is on her knees, covering the skull and hat with dirt until only the poppies are sticking out.

What a waste of a good hat.

The trench grows shallower until it turns back into flat ground, as though the soldiers grew too tired to dig anymore. Emilie grabs me by the wrist and pulls me back toward the main road, muttering about how we never should have strayed from it. It isn't long before we go over a hill and see the smoking chimneys of Courties on the other side.

Grandmère says Courties has been there just as long as France, if not much longer. She tells us it was once a rich village where many people lived, back when we fought the English instead of the Germans. Emilie says that is all fool's talk, and that it has always been as miserable as it was then. For once, I think Emilie was right.

Twenty little stone houses are clustered in the valley, placed wherever there is room for them. Nearly all of them face the church, which stands above them all, as it should. The gray bricks have turned very dark and worn, and the steeple went missing long ago, but it still looks finer than the rest of the village. I wish the Germans would come and blow it away with one of their great machines. Then, I think, I would not have to visit such a dreadful place any longer.

Emilie is much too good at reading my face. "Look cheerful, Alfred," she says. "Don't you want Father Duchamp to treat you well?"

"Not really…"

She scowls. "Then at least try to stay quiet this time."

It is dark inside the church. The curtains have all been drawn shut, so the light will not hurt the sick and the wounded. Because it is not Sunday, the church has become part of Madame Thierry's hospital. The benches have all been pushed aside to make room for cots and blankets. Everything smells of Armagnac brandy and dead flesh. Ladies from town move from cot to cot, checking the bodies that lie there and sometimes covering a face. No one ever speaks to anybody.

The only voices come from the other side of the room, where a lady and a man are whispering to each other. The lady is very small and made of wrinkles, and she wears her white hair without a lock out of place. The man is younger but frightens me much more. Everything about him is gray, like the statue of Mary behind the altar: even his eyes are gray all over, for they see nothing. Yet his head still turns at the sound of Emilie's step. He expects her at the same time each week. "Mademoiselle Jacquinot? Is that you?"

"*Oui.*" Emilie lets me go, walks up to him, and curtsies. "*Bonjour, monsieur.* Madame Thierry." She clasps the handle of the basket and looks down at her dirty boots, so she does not have to look at the old woman.

Grandmère never has anything good to say about Madame Thierry. At first Emilie and I did not understand: were they not the same sort of woman? Grandmère collected food and clothes for the needy; Madame collected medicine. Her grand stone house on the edge of the valley had been a hospital for as long as we could remember. She was doing good, was she not?

Grandmère snorted at us when we asked her that. "Oh, Madame certainly does good," she said, "if you're on the right side of her grudges."

In time we understood what she meant. Madame's rooms were never quite as full as they could have been. Officers who found their way to Courties from the prison camps were greeted with the softest beds and the closest care — if they were French. All the others were spread out through whatever was left. If they had been given the Treatment, she sent them away and made them rest in the church or her barn. Whenever sickness swept through the village, it was always the poorer families — those who had spoken ill of her in the past — for whom there was not enough time or medicine to spare.

Madame Thierry's dark eyes glare out at Emilie from her puckered face. "Do you have the laudanum?" she says. Her voice is like stones rubbing against one another.

"*Oui, madame.*" Emilie reaches into her basket and hands Madame a little brown bottle.

Madame snatches it away, peers at what is inside. "That is all?"

"*Grandmère* does not withhold from you. You know that." Emilie looks up at Madame, letting her see her frown.

Madame's grip on the handle of her cane tightens and then grows loose once more. She stows the laudanum somewhere in the folds of her black dress.

"Alfred! Come give Father Duchamp your basket!" Emilie says as she hands her own to the old priest. "All the rest is for you."

I drag myself forward and thrust out my arm, taking care not to look at Father Duchamp. Emilie glares down and gives my ankle a little kick, but the Father did not seem to notice nor care that I am being rude. He takes my basket, smiling at me and putting a hand on my head. "*Merci beaucoup,* Alfred."

I step away. He is too close — besides, it is Grandmère he should be thanking and not me.

"Do you need anything back at the farm, *mademoiselle?*" Father Duchamp says to Emilie.

"No…" Emilie looks around the room.

"Is something wrong?"

"Is Billy still here, *monsieur?*"

Father Duchamp's face turns solemn as he nods, then points to a cot in the corner.

Billy Green is his name. He first came here three years ago, running from a camp the Germans had locked him up in. But no cages could hold him, he said with pride. Not an American. He had bright eyes and a crooked grin. He lived in the church and helped at our farm sometimes because he wanted to make Emilie smile, and it worked.

One night he vanished. A few months later, he came wandering back, and only Emilie could recognize him. He was wearing a German uniform. He never said why. He never said anything at all after that. His skin has gone gray, his eyes dull. His breaths are shallow, as if it hurts to take them. I don't know why it would; all he does is lie on his cot and stare at the ceiling.

"It's because he's trying to remember Heaven," the ladies who tend to him tell me. "He was given the Treatment too many times, you see."

I once asked Grandmère what the Treatment was and what it did to men: she spit on the ground and shook her head. Emilie said that no one besides the scientists really knew what the Treatment was, and that it wouldn't be proper to speak of what it did.

"Of course you would say that; you're a girl!" I told her. "The older boys will tell me if I ask them."

"Go and ask them, then. Don't come to me when you wish you hadn't."

All the boys who are nearly grown up live outside of town in a hidden camp that the men built. If you are old and strong enough, you go there and learn all about fighting in the war, and if you learn well, they sneak you across the lines to go kill Germans. Someday I will go, I hope.

At first the boys told me the Treatment was a government secret; they'd be locked up if they told anyone. When I gave them a few coins and swore I wouldn't breathe a word of it, then they told me everything they knew.

"When you die out on the front," they said, "the scientists come and take your body to a laboratory in the city. Then they work on you to make you better."

"I heard they put a shock through your brain to wake you up!"

"*Non,* I think it's a serum they put in your blood."

"It's both! I've seen it done."

"But what does it do to you?" I asked.

"You come alive again," the oldest of the boys whispered. "And when you do, you're stronger, and you don't have to eat and won't get sick. Nothing can kill you but a bullet, so you get to do the important jobs once you're sent back to the front."

"And what happens if a bullet gets you?"

"They're supposed to let you be," one of them said. "But they can do it again if you signed a form. Sometimes they make you sign it. Then they can keep bringing you back as long as they have you in one piece."

"I hope they do!" said another. "I think it would be grand to fight Germans over and over and see them be frightened of you!"

In the church, Emilie sits down beside the cot and takes Billy Green's hand, as she has done so often. He does not seem to know she is there; if he does know, he does not care to look at her, and that is not like him at all. Emilie combs his ragged brown hair and straightens his blankets. *"Je suis desole,"* she whispers. "I am very sorry."

Why should she feel sorry for him? He came over here to fight in the war because he wanted to, didn't he? Besides, Grandmère says that tears do no one any good.

"There will be troops marching over the main road," Father Duchamp tells Emilie as we prepare to leave town. "You will be safer if you go through the forest."

So, we walk north, past the tents on the edge of town and out of the valley. One moment there are no trees, and the next they are everywhere. Emilie says this is one of the last old forests in France. It is all that Courties has for a wall, so they have never cut it down for firewood.

It is dark and quiet inside. The branches and leaves keep out the sun and the birds have all gone away. There is the cold wind, and the snap of twigs beneath my feet. There are stranger noises as well, the cries of horses and the rumble of wheels.

I want to see what is happening, so I pull myself away from Emilie and try to climb the nearest tree. Emilie pulls me back down just as quick. "Not by yourself, you aren't." She makes me hold her basket and goes up first, stepping from one branch to another. I follow when she is too far ahead to stop me.

Emilie is sitting on the tallest branch, a hand keeping the sun from her eyes as she looks about. She suddenly stops, and her hand flies to her mouth.

"What is it?" I say as I sit down beside her.

"Hush!" she whispers and points.

They are cutting their way through the woods and coming toward us, a long line of men dressed in the Kaiser's gray. There must be hundreds of them! Coming back from the front, I supposed. They look as though they have seen fighting. They hang their heads and bend beneath the packs they carry, and most of them are missing their funny little helmets. Their horses are thin, and the wagons they pull are filled with dead and wounded men. No one says a word, except to pass on an order.

One man happens to glance at our tree and sees the basket I left by its trunk. Then he looks up into the branches, right at me. I want to make a rude gesture at him, but Emilie stops my hand and casts him a wicked look instead. *Keep walking,* she seems to say with her eyes. *You have no business here.*

He seems to understand, perhaps even agree; he lowers his head once more and is lost in the gray sea of marchers.

They file on for a few more minutes before the line begins to grow more scattered and comes to an end at last. By now the sun has gone, covered up by dark storm clouds. Fat, cold raindrops pour down on our heads, but Emilie does not move. Instead she waits until the last of the soldiers is far away before she lets me climb down. We start for home once more in silence; with one hand, Emilie holds her coat above her head to keep away the rain, and with the other, she pulls me along by my wrist. Every few seconds she looks behind us.

All of a sudden, she stops, listens, and clutches her basket as though she would like to throw it. "Run when I tell you to," she whispers.

I look where she was pointing, toward a cluster of trees and bushes. Something tall and thin is in the shadows, moving toward us. Something shaped like a man.

Emilie shoves me down the path and runs after me as the man comes stumbling toward us, groaning and pressing a hand to his side. She grabs a rock and turns around to throw it. The man stops, raises an arm, and yells out to us. His voice is that of a German, yet he speaks in broken French. "Please wait!"

It takes us by surprise, and we stop without meaning to. Emilie takes a step forward, the rock still in her hands. "Who's there?"

The man is able to walk into the light before his legs fail him. It is the German from before, who looked up at us in the tree. Why, he is not a man at all! He is barely older than either of us! Blood is coming out of a wound in his side faster than his dirty bandage and hands can keep it in. He trembles and whimpers, but after a while he crawls toward me and speaks. "I need…your help…"

Emilie takes my hand, and we kneel at the German boy's side. When she tries to take off the bandage, he pushes her hands away.

"You'll die if you don't let me take a look at it," she says.

"I know." A bit of color seems to come back into his gray face as he thinks of it. "Please bury me where Commander will not find me. I do not want to come back. Not again,"

Something about this feels very wrong. "Shouldn't we tell someone, Emilie?"

"We aren't going to."

"But he's a German!"

The German boy is looking at me now. There is fear in his eyes. "They will send me back to the front if you tell. This way I shall not hurt you good people any longer. You want to kill a German, yes? Now you can."

Emilie speaks, because now I cannot. "We will help you. We promise."

The German boy smiles. "Thank you." He takes one last shuddering breath. By now he has stopped moving, and his skin has gone all gray once more. The flesh begins to stiffen and crumble, falling away from the bones. I touch his cheek; it comes away in her hand and then turns to dust.

Emilie stops me as I stand up to run. "You can help, Alfred."

It is half an hour before we make our way out of the woods. We bury what is left of the German boy under a tree and carve a little cross in the bark. Emilie says a few prayers. I stand as far away as I can without angering her, shifting from one foot to the other. At last she stands, but she does not move away.

I tug on the sleeve of her dress. *"Grandmère* is waiting for us, Emilie."

"I want to stay here a moment longer."

"But the German's dead, isn't he?"

Emilie kneels in front of me and takes my hands. "Alfred," she says, "you must promise never to tell anyone about this, for our sake and his. Do you understand?"

"What if someone finds out?"

"Then they will tell you that you've done a very bad thing, and you must remember that they are wrong. Can you do that?"

I don't know what to say, so I decide to say nothing at all.

Grandmère does not look up when we step through the door of the farmhouse. "Your lunch is cold," she says.

"Pardon, Grandmère," says Emilie. "We had to wait for the road to clear."

Grandmère nods. She already knows we would rather not talk of whatever it is, and neither would she. We eat our cold lunch, and then Emilie leaves to work in the garden. I climb up to my room and try to forget the boy in the woods. The day passes us by and ends without another word.

On most evenings, I am quick to fall asleep, but tonight there is no such luck. Each time I close my eyes, I can only see the German boy's crumbling face. After a few hours, I crawl out of bed and sneak downstairs.

Emilie and Grandmère share a bedroom. Grandmère is already snoring, but Emilie is still awake, reading a book by the light of a nearly melted candle. She looks up and raises her eyebrows as she sees me in the doorway. "What is it, Alfred?"

"May I stay with you a little while?"

Emilie frowns but closes her book and pats the end of the bed. I sit down, hug my knees, and stare at the wall.

"You're thinking about the German boy." It is not a question.

"Emilie…" I am not sure how to begin. "What was it like before all of this?"

"What do you mean?"

"I mean before the war. Do you remember much?"

Emilie gets out of bed and sits down beside me. "I remember clear skies and good harvests and warm fires in the winter. I know Mama liked to smile and laugh, and Papa worked hard for us. And it was quiet. It was always so quiet." Now she is staring off at the wall too.

"Do you think the German boy is in Heaven now?"

"I hope he is."

"What happened to him and to Billy…" I take a breath. "It won't happen to me, will it?"

Emilie does not say a thing. She only puts her arms around me and cries until the morning comes.

XOXOX XOXOX XOXOX X

About the Author

Dana Himrich is about to graduate from the University of Tulsa with degrees in history and English. She plans to continue writing fantasy/sci-if stories once she is done with school. *Poppy Lane* is her third publication. She lives just outside of Tulsa with her parents, brother, and cat.

Bliss

S.B. Roark

It was called Bliss. A bright, woad-blue "B" embossed in the middle of a square of moisture-adhesive tape, pressed between two thin sheets of protective, clear plastic. The sigil dripped flecks of inky blood from the corners of its consonant. This "bite" was its trademark. A warning meant to keep little kids from confusing it for one of those fake tattoos from the candy machine. As if the price tag wasn't deterrent enough.

Shelby got her first pair of patches off one of the boys at the bus stop who she knew from community college. The pock-faced dealer had laughed in the middle of his soft-sell when she'd nervously pulled her savings out of her fanny pack. In between snickers, he said he'd give her a two-for-one, fat girl special, as it might be the only chance at a good time she'd ever get. She didn't have the sass to tell him off. He was probably right.

The absinthe she'd swiped from the grocery store breathed licorice-scented sighs from the goblet on the windowsill of her bedroom. In the gaudy light of twilight, the fluid inside the chunky, green Goodwill find looked almost like a proper fairy's potion. Next to it sat the remnants of her deep-fried dinner: some cheese curls and a half-eaten chicken drumstick left to congeal as an offering for any spirits who might wish to partake in its greasy rite.

With cheese-encrusted, hazard-orange fingers, Shelby removed her polo shirt and padded bra. The greyish flesh of her exposed breasts hung limply against the mound of fat that dominated the territory from her bust to her thighs. Only that engorged shelf of cellulite propped-up the tired, pigeon titties that might have otherwise dangled lifeless down the bulbous cascade of her fat. Even in the dim, hallowed light of twilight, they looked more like squeezed-empty sacks than the voluptuous symbols of womanhood they were supposed to be.

Shelby detested getting undressed. At school, she was known as the Layered Lesbo because she wore her step aerobics outfit beneath her regular clothes to save herself from having to change in front of the others. Worse than the taunts and snickers was the sweaty collection of clothes she had to endure beneath her outfit for the rest of the school day. By lunch time, she smelled like an old, wet boot.

With her grandfather's blood-testing pen, Shelby pierced two tiny holes into the skin in the upper-right portion of her left breast. She watched with perverse satisfaction as a duo of tiny pinpricks of blood oozed from the holes to issue a stinging complaint against their freedom. The sticky drops looked impossibly scarlet in the jaundiced light of the candle's flame. Exposed, the warm trickle cooled quickly upon her breast. Staring at it made her feel nervous and excited at the same time, like an Amazon who'd sawed-off her own teat, ready to go into battle, bow drawn.

Shelby peeled away the protective sleeves of plastic from one of the squares of Bliss and dunked it into the goblet. The cloudy green liquor blurred the bold lines of the letter and distorted the bite into a pair of ashy teardrops. She removed the absinthe-anointed tattoo from its baptism and carefully placed the tiny square over her wound like a balm. Or a sacrament.

A day's worth of sweat suffused the territories where flesh pressed against flesh with a heavy, pungent odor. It mingled now with the scent of licorice spirits, cheap vanilla tallow, and the oily tang of fried food. Shelby reclined into the well-worn recesses of her futon and kicked off the denim length of her wide-leg jeans, her white cotton bloomers tangled-up in the recess of her crotch seam.

Her cartoon-themed alarm clock glowed a bleary seven from the bedside table. She waited, tonguing the oil-slick remnant of her meal against the roof of her mouth with hungry impatience.

The poorly sealed window frame allowed gusts of evening chill to percolate across her skin. Where fall breeze met flesh, goose-pimples erupted with a painful fervor and seemed to push-out new lengths of course, dark hair across her body.

She'd wanted to wait above the covers, let the night steal into the room like a lover to find her naked and ready as in the romance novels she hoarded beneath her bed, but shivers made her retreat. Underneath the layers of flannel blankets, the lure of sleep proved too strong to ignore. She drifted off as the candle guttered in its pool of tallow, flared brightly once, and then died out.

Shelby awoke with a start.

She lay atop a mound of furs swollen from more than half a dozen kills. The tickling hairs itched across her skin with an unfamiliar caress. Over her stretched the greatest of the hides, an impossibly large, long-haired sable pelt, whose heaviness urged her back into her bed with the promise of warm indulgence.

Shelby passed a tentative hand over a swath of its silken fur. The pelt was soft beneath her touch, the smooth lengths of individual hairs each undeniably real. Wherever she was, it was no mere dream.

Firelight from a well-stoked hearth danced across the stone walls of the large chamber and filled the room with the pungent scent of cedar. Shelby sat up and pushed the fur off of her, only to blush in embarrassment. She was naked underneath.

Yet, that was not all the motion revealed. Shelby stared down in awe. Her frame was slender and lithe, composed of smooth, taut expanses of creamy skin. Large breasts mounded her chest into twin mountains divided by a steep ravine of cleavage. She ran a shaky hand over them and thrilled as fingers tumbled over the large, pebble-like nipples at their pinnacle. The soft pink nubs hardened beneath her clumsy, inexperienced touch.

Shelby cast about the strange, semi-circular stone room for a mirror; she just *had* to see herself. Only age-worn tapestries and a soot-rimmed coat of arms hung upon the walls. Besides the makeshift bed and a pair of honey-colored chairs that clustered around a small table, there was little else in the way of furniture.

She rose tentatively and tiptoed to the thin gash of a window that allowed a shaft of pale moonlight to spill across the well-worn wooden floor. Face pressed into the arrow-slit, Shelby could just make out the midnight-blue shadows of a garden stretched out far below her.

Cool spring air quickened through the tiny gap and splayed breezy fingered through her long, unbound hair. The gust carried up to her the myriad scents of a well-tended green-space. Shelby trembled against the chilly onslaught. From somewhere nearby, a river mumbled an icy lullaby.

The chamber door banged open, startling Shelby away from her perch. She glanced over and her breath caught. A stunning man dominated the wide expanse inside the threshold.

Wayward blond hair fell, careless, down the long, exposed length of his upper body. His chest was broad. His muscles, sweat-slickened, shone a burnished gold in the firelight. Arctic-blue eyes swept over her, through her. The suggestive stare ravaged her thoughts until she was dazed in the presence of his obvious passion.

He looked as though he had just stepped off the cover of one of Shelby's bodice-rippers; the image of a man forgotten, too barbaric and bloodthirsty to survive in modern day. He was a thing of pure fantasy, a Viking from myth and legend.

He spoke. The rumble of words was garbled, foreign, in a language just on this side of familiar. But his motions were universal; he strode toward her with a cocky assurance that proclaimed that his intent was not to be denied.

Shelby shrank away from him and tried to cover herself with the feeble drape of her arms. The cool stones of the wall licked a trail of ice across her back, and she arched away from it with a yelp. The man stopped less than a pace before her and inclined his head.

She blushed, and he smiled at her bashfulness.

With deliberate slowness, he reached out a hand and wrapped it around Shelby's, prying away her veil of modesty with even, steady pressure. With her hand in his, he pulled it toward him and splayed her palm across his bare chest, covering it with his own.

Shelby's breath caught at the impossible reality of his form, the warmness of his skin, the steady drumbeat of his heart beneath her hand.

"Who are you?" she asked. Her voice was strange, not her own, but was instead something soft and sultry.

His only response was to take a step toward the pile of furs, ferrying her along after him in his wake. Fear lanced through Shelby but something else too. Something exhilarating and feminine and like nothing she had ever felt before.

The Viking knelt and urged her down into the waiting recess of the still-warm pelts. His primal fragrance crackled against her senses, and her mind fogged with delirious arousal. Where once he had been clad in trousers and boots, suddenly there was nothing to separate him from her touch. He eased fully next to her and wrapped himself around her willing form. He felt like magic: warm and heady and impossible to deny.

They kissed for what must have been hours until the unfamiliar action began to feel natural. Finally, when the first hints of dawn threatened to dispel the dreamy atmosphere of the room, they joined.

Shelby had expected some kind of pain. Wasn't the first time with a man supposed to hurt? True, she'd done the deed herself some time ago, speared into her womanhood and quested till pain announced its destination. She'd broken herself in, eager not to suffer any longer under the cloud of undesirable purity. Nobody liked an inexperienced woman. Virginity was just another sign of weakness.

Afterward, she had waddled, quiet as a mouse, to the downstairs bathroom. In her grandparents' cast iron tub, she'd sat until the hot water had grown cold and turned pink on her own plucked rose.

But it'd been worth it. No one could laugh behind her back anymore. No more hurtful slights about rotten peaches or circling fruit flies. She'd broken herself in like a warrior. She'd made herself a woman.

When her Viking took her, there was no lingering discomfort, no sense that his pleasure came at the unfair cost of her pain. There was only her intense need to be wanted and his voracious desire to be invited back. With the fierce press of his kisses, he nipped at the succor of her breast and held her, vise-like, while she clung to him, afraid to let go.

* * *

The alarm clock rang at eight the next morning, ripping her out of the last vestiges of the dream. With shaky arms, Shelby peeled the sweat-heavy layers of blankets away. An all too familiar gluttonous blob of human waste greeted her eyes. Shelby lay in the quickly cooling remnants of her private passion and wept.

The rest of the day proceeded in a blur. Fatigue, heavier than any she had ever known, found her listless and unable to eat. Grandma insisted her pale face and hints of fever meant flu-season had come early. Shelby submitted, too tired to put up a fuss, to rub-downs of mentholated ointments and tinctures of orange juice and saltpeter.

That night, Shelby stared at the remnants of her ritual. The sickly-sweet licorice alcohol, the puddle of yellow tallow that had once been a candle, and the tiny sleeves of cellophane, still slightly blued from the Bliss it had once contained…they all seemed pathetic and childish somehow. She shook her too-heavy head, steeped in the numbing effects of the cold medicine she'd been forced to take, and sighed.

This wasn't right. It wasn't proper courting.

Shelby collapsed into her bed, too exhausted to cover herself with the blankets. If she was going to try again, she'd need a better set-up. She couldn't very well invite her new boyfriend back into her boudoir until she had something worthy of his arrival. Even if she sold all her things, the TV, the nightstands, her entire collection of vintage Nancy Drew books, that would hardly pay for a proper bed and mattress combo, not to mention more Bliss-tickets to date night.

She only had the one left, and already the urge to use it was hard to ignore. What would she do when necessity overrode willpower and she finally submitted? How would she get her next fix? She'd need to come up with a plan to get a lot of money. And fast.

Being a large girl meant that when Shelby wore an oversized jacket on top of a couple of layers of clothes, the store manager couldn't tell with just a glance that her bulk concealed a small collection of his stock. She'd tucked the black silk sheet set below her tummy, held in place by the overworked elastic of her pants; the oil warmer balanced atop that. Even with the obscuring lines of her downy jacket, she kept her gut sucked in tight to make the hard edges of her pilfered goods appear more natural. But damn if she didn't feel as if she was burning alive! By the time she was ready to make her escape, the sweat rolled down her face in eye-stinging rivulets.

She held her breath as she passed the cashier's counter and silently counted the steps toward the exit.

"I'm sorry you were unable to find what you were looking for," the manager at the till expressed with false concern, startling Shelby out of her basic math.

She nodded over at him and grinned. She tried for a "thank you," or a "no worries," but both wanted to be said at the same time. Instead of coherent words, all that came out of Shelby's mouth was a toneless, garbled grunt.

The man glanced up at her from the recesses of his over-sized encyclopedia, which did little to hide the girly magazine within.

Shelby's cheeks flared with heat. If she could just make it a few more feet, she'd be scot-free. She ducked her head and quickened her pace.

And ran straight into the large frame of the store's security guard.

Strong hands grabbed her upper arms as she rebounded from the collision, the packages hidden under her clothes tumbling onto the floor.

"You just hold on right there, missy," the guard ordered as he eyed the goods. He tightened his grip into something painful. "You're coming with me. I think we'd better have a little talk in the back room, don't you?"

The security guard stared down at her with bored, indifferent eyes. Age had made the slight weight which he must have born on his once younger frame bloom into full huskiness. It now pushed apart the bottom three buttons of his shirt with irate resentment.

Shelby tilted her head back to continue her bored perusal. His flat, blonde hair thinned at the brow like a meager tree-line and allowed a clear view into the acres of sparse foliage within. Only his breath was animated past the point of blandness and assaulted her nostrils with the almost physical slap of acidic, day-old coffee.

"What were you doing with those items under your clothing?" he asked.

Shelby hunched further into the plastic bowl of her chair and stared once more at the blue buttons of the guard's shirt.

The security guard slammed a meaty fist against the back wall with a loud thud, ripping Shelby out of her idle apathy. She jumped and glanced back up into his face.

"Do you think this is some kind of game?" he growled, collections of white spittle gathering into the corners of his mouth.

Shelby shrugged and worried at a hunk of chapped lip flesh with the edges of her teeth until it became a long bit of skin to chew. It'd be pointless to bother with the guard's question. His lines felt well-rehearsed; more narration than conversation.

In full swing of his performance, it could have been anyone taking this heat right now. Nothing she'd say would matter.

"This is no game!" he answered for her, feeding the scrap of dialogue to her to try to keep the repartee flowing. Between the two, Shelby's chewy skin flap was more appetizing a morsel to swallow.

At Shelby's continued silence, he leaned forward and squinted coal-dark eyes down at her. His gaze rested heavy on her face past the point of natural withdrawal, the intimidating move obviously his work-horse. Shelby was the first to look away.

She shrugged again. She'd been caught shoplifting. What more was there to say?

"What did you need…" the security guard looked over to the pile of things on the desk which had recently been beneath Shelby's coat, "sheets and some candles for?"

"An oil warmer," she corrected.

"Whatever," he barked. "So why were these things so important that you felt you had to become a criminal to get them?"

Shelby sighed. "They're for my boyfriend."

"Your what?" Disbelief dripped from the question like molasses off a biscuit. "*You* have a boyfriend?"

She crossed her arms, suddenly intent upon the flecks of mud on the tops of her foam clogs. What did this guy know about love anyway? He was a walking, talking bachelor flat with a fridge full of canned beer and one-dollar Salisbury steak dinners. Someone like him could never understand the deep bond she shared with her beloved. It was easier to let him doubt.

She flicked her gaze to his left hand. No ring. It wasn't like *he* mattered to anyone, anyway.

The security guard frowned. "Did you meet him on the internets or something?"

She was saved from giving a response when the door to the back office opened, and her grandmother walked in. Shelby stood, forcing the cop to back up a pace or risk bumping bellies with her. He wisely conceded space.

Even with her head bowed, Shelby could feel the heavy weight of Gran-gran's disapproval like a sound rap on her crown. She tried to shy out from under her gaze, but the smaller woman bird-dogged her from across the tiny room, her glare so sharp it could have been fashioned out of broken glass. It made the guard's stare feel like a kid's attempt at make-believe. It'd be years before age honed his spite into something so sour it rivaled vinegar. For now, Gran-gran alone held that distinction.

"That's my granddaughter," the older woman stated as she pointed at Shelby with a small, lace-gloved finger. Shelby tried not to flinch but the response seemed engraved into her psyche. Even in her Sunday best, with her fullest wig, Gran-gran could still intimidate the bejesus out of her. "What kind of trouble has she found for herself?"

The security guard stood at attention. Shelby's grandmother just had that kind of effect on people.

"Well, ma'am…" he began, clearing his throat with a cough. "This young lady was caught trying to illegally procure these items," he gestured to the pile of packages, "by concealing them on her person."

Shelby watched warily as Gran-gran glanced over at the sheet set and oil warmer. She picked up the latter.

"What's this for?" she asked no one in particular.

"Candles or something," the guard answered with feigned interest.

"It's an oil warmer," Shelby corrected automatically. At her grandmother's squint, she bit her tongue.

"I see," the older woman stated. "So my Shelby tried her hand at thieving and failed. Now what? Does she have to pay some kind of fine or something?"

The security guard brought a hand up to rub at the back of his neck. "Well…" he began, drawing out the word as if putting a great deal of thought into the question. "Since this is her first time trying something like this…this is your first time, right?" he demanded of Shelby.

She managed a few nods.

"And since she was caught before she managed to get away with anything…" the security guard continued, "I guess I could let her go with a warning. So long as she can provide me with a reasonable explanation for why she chose to behave in this inappropriate way."

Shelby glanced at him. His smile cut across his mouth like the blade of a sickle. He wanted her to restate the boyfriend thing, wanted a family member to prove that her story was pure hokum.

But she wouldn't do it. She wouldn't risk her grandmother finding out about her beloved and somehow coming between them. Gran-gran would never believe that Shelby's love was a real, living, breathing reality. So instead, she fibbed.

"I don't have a good excuse," she supplied. "Because there is no good excuse for what I did. Stealing is wrong, and I'm sorry." This last bit she directed at Gran-gran. If she was going to issue an apology, it was best to make it count.

Gran-gran looked her over with an appraising eye as she scratched her scalp to readjust her wig. After a few moments, she nodded.

"All right then. Let's get you home."

The security guard made room for Shelby as she bustled past. She lingered in the open doorway as her grandmother turned to him.

"I want to thank you for calling me and for the kindness you've shown my Shelby. And don't worry," she added, voice brittle and jagged as chips of lead paint, "she'll get a whooping for this; I don't care how old she is."

Shelby's cheeks burned, and she looked away. The security guard's response was smug, full of a sureness that only self-righteousness could give.

"No trouble at all, ma'am," he crowed with swollen bravado. "All in a day's work."

Gran-gran waited until the two of them were out in the parking lot to let loose her tongue-lashing.

"You wait till your grandpa hears about this," she threatened, voice dangerously soft.

Shelby stifled a groan. If she thought the humiliation of having her grandmother called was bad, the threat of her grandfather's wrath left a sour taste of bile at the back of her throat. Gramps was old school about his discipline, and Shelby had born many the belt marks to verify his zeal. He'd be none too happy to hear about how she'd once again disgraced the family name. It didn't matter if she was twenty-two or sixty-two, he'd let her have it. Shelby'd be lucky if she would be able to sit down ever again.

"The shame of me getting such a call and having to come down here for this," Gran-gran continued. "Why did you do such an idiotic thing, girl? If you wanted something so bad, why didn't you just go buy it?"

"I don't have any money," Shelby mumbled.

"Are you brain damaged or something? Why couldn't you go out and *earn* some like regular people…save up for the things you want?"

Shelby shrugged and fell into step behind her grandmother. She doubted now would be a good time to ask for an allowance.

"I'm sorry," she repeated. In the end, there was no excuse Shelby could give that Gran-gran would understand.

"What you need is a job," Gran-gran announced. "That will keep you out of trouble and give you some running-around money. Even a dunderhead like you could manage both school and something part-time. When we get home, I'm gonna talk to Gramps about it, see if he can't set you up with something at his shop. That should give you some pocket change and keep you out of trouble at the same time."

Shelby sighed. There went her free time. With Gramps as her jailor, she'd be under his watch after school and on the weekends. At least this could mean she'd start getting paid for a job she'd been on-again, off-again helping out with for years. Well…maybe.

Gramps never let go of a nickel he didn't have to and that included not paying family for their time. If the old man didn't come through, she'd have to get real inventive when it came to filling her pockets.

Gran-gran must have taken her silence for regret because she stopped to glance back at her.

"You want me to go through the drive-through on our way home?" she offered, a bit of honey mixing into her unsweetened lemonade tone. "Maybe get you a soft-serve cone?"

At the mention of fast food, Shelby paled. She hadn't eaten anything in almost two days, and just the thought made her stomach pitch a fit. She took a few shallow breaths and tried to force her belly to calm. Shelby doubted there'd be anything in there to come back up, but she wasn't too eager to test the notion.

"Huh…" Granny said, eyeing her. "Don't like that idea too much, do you? Well," she said, turning back around to pick up the pace, "at least that's one good thing about you getting sick. Maybe you'll lose some weight. As my mother always told me, stomach flu is a girl's best friend."

At home, Gran-gran kept her mouth shut about Shelby's little trek into the criminal world. Whatever her reasons for not sharing, she kept quiet about those too. The incident soon became just one more thing grandmother and granddaughter didn't talk about, like periods and boys and bullies.

Shelby didn't look forward to the inevitable hiding she'd get if Gran-gran got a hair across her ass and blabbed to Gramps. So as not to tempt fate, when not in school or at her new part-time job, she cloistered herself in her room.

But that wasn't a bad thing. The solitude allowed her to get her bedroom make-over done in under a week. The futon was replaced by a larger, more adult queen-sized bed she'd found on Craigslist and had delivered, evolving the room into a place purely for rest and romance.

The solitary piece of furniture dominated the attic room and left little space for anything else. Luckily, there wasn't anything else in the room besides a small stack of poetry and mythology books with a tray on top for some candles. Even the walls had been given a new coat of oxblood red, with Shelby working into the wee hours peeling and scraping away the old wallpaper like skin from a sunburned back.

The transformation had taken its toll, though. With the strange sickness still heavy upon her, just getting through school proved a momentous task. Her days were spent in a constant haze, with Shelby making it to her classes more out of rote than anything else. She had no energy, just a strange kind of hunger, a passion which urged her ever forward like a siren's song. Only the thought of Him gave her the strength to complete her bedroom overhaul. Somehow she knew He would be pleased.

Eating was also still a problem. Shelby managed to choke down one of her grandfather's nutrition drinks a day, but besides that, she faltered. The whole idea of consuming anything upset her, and she didn't dare get started on the gross-out idea of chowing down on rotting carcasses, or as her grandparents liked to call them, meat products.

Maybe she had become a vegan. Could someone grow into something like that? All she did know was that her pants were fitting looser, and her shirts didn't cling to her fat rolls as they once did.

She wasn't the only one to notice, either. Other kids at college, normally losers and bullies, were more and more often silent around her as opposed to viciously opinionated. Even the new hairstyle she'd scrounged the last of her cash up for had met with, if not rave reviews, at least quiet contemplation.

Shelby wasn't dumb enough to call this change in people's attitudes acceptance, but whatever found her less humiliated was a win in her book. She even began to change clothes for step aerobics class. Who cared what stupid people thought of her body? The only opinion that mattered was His.

She made it to Saturday before her willpower gave out.

It'd been almost two weeks since that first time, and Shelby was jonesing for another date. Every night she'd dreamt of Him, but only in vague snippets of that pure, perfect moment: the cool press of stone against her back, the scent of the river-bordered garden, the warm caress of skin against skin.

She'd wanted to draw out the pain until it'd become something close to pleasure, a sweet temptation to which she would eventually succumb. But that first beautiful dream had soon become a haunted memory: the garbled after images she endured each night like pieces to a puzzle she couldn't quite recreate. Her newly painted bedroom sat refurnished but empty of a soul, a bower without a blushing bride.

She had no money. She had no prospects. All she had was one more bite of Bliss.

It was so easy to give in.

That night he was a poet. A pale, troubled soul with raven's wing hair that framed his brow with a careless abandon. His lips were thin; no…they were full and guarded save the unspoken words of his latest poetic creation. His were the hands of an artist, with long fingers firm enough to form the most delicate of intricacies in clay, or powerful enough to while away the hours producing melodies on his guitar, no wait…his violin.

The top few buttons of his white blouse were undone and lent him a cavalier air, inviting the eye to skim over his creamy, pale skin at leisure. Shelby waited, taking him in. Wanting him to notice her, needing him to need her as much as she did him.

He did not look at her directly but gazed almost lazily at her from beneath the long jet length of his eyelashes. With a haughty distain, he eyed her briefly and then looked away. His cursory glance all but dismissed her before she'd even gotten a chance to speak.

Shelby's stomach tightened, the obvious rejection souring the moment. But as if he could sense the turn in the mood, he glanced up at her fully. A cocky, yet self-effacing smile appeared on his full, pouty lips, and he held out a hand. It arched, palm down, towards her. She didn't know if she was supposed to shake it or kiss it.

"Are you here to pose for a sketch?" he asked, his voice dulcet and tickled across her senses like butterfly kisses.

The weight of his focus seemed to press upon her chest, making it hard to breathe. She'd never seen anyone so painfully beautiful before. Not in his previous form had he looked so much like a fallen angel: wings clipped, feathers bloody.

"You're rather late," he complained, once again putting her on edge. "I had expected you some time ago. Now, all of the good light has gone."

"I am sorry," she said quickly. The apology was habitual, and the tang of humility tasted well-worn and drab on her lips, like stale crackers or over-steeped tea.

"Well, you are here now," he supplied graciously. "And I am sure I can think of *some* way for you to make it up to me."

A shiver coursed up Shelby's spine as she took his hand, silently acquiescing to whatever plans would see her back in his graces. He took her there on the sofa, with no preamble or sweet words. His was a desperate hunger which her selfishness had too long denied.

Her love delighted in conquest that night and flayed open her ponderous apprehensions to strip her bare of her humility. Shelby came to understand that there was no room for questions in this love affair. Or defenses.

Hers were useless fears, anchors of societal control designed to keep her low, malleable by everyone around her. He would master her. He would set her free, but only if she gave herself fully over to the concept of Him.

With cold intent, he analyzed her. Reformed the useless clay of her flesh and made it warm once more. He tore her down to nothing only to build her back up again into something pure, something needed.

His love was an acid, a tool for etching glass, giving design to otherwise transparent arranged sand. To be his muse was a crucible and an honor. He would take all he could from his vessel and use it to shore himself up, bleeding her dry with his never-ending need. And she would submit beneath Him. She had to. She would do anything for love.

Payday at Gramp's warehouse proved a good place to pick up some easy dough. The undocumented workers got stiffed no later than four o'clock by their ridiculously low wages, and by four-thirty, they were lining up behind the building near the back fence, ready to get stiff again.

Shelby didn't want for disgruntled customers looking to blow off some steam. She figured, despite her looks, the thought of sticking it to the boss through the boss' granddaughter was all the aphrodisiac the men needed. More often than not, she was right.

They couldn't seem to wait to position themselves before her, legs akimbo, urging her with rough, callused hands, to get to work. Mouth filled with them, the musky taste of sour sweat and machine grease invaded her senses, making her gag. This made the men work faster, thrust back harder, confusing the sound of her vomit reflex with a capacity warning. Whatever delusion made them finish quickly so she could go on to the next guy was fine by her. In the end, it all boiled down to fantasy.

No one took longer than a few minutes, and no one stayed afterward to help her off her knees. They just dropped the money onto the ground, already limp from exertion, and walked away. But Shelby didn't mind. When she was through with those that came, she had enough money for another couple of date nights, and that was all that mattered.

Sunrise was still a distant threat against the blue-black sky when Shelby arrived at the bus stop Friday morning. She waited, pacing a perimeter around the trash-strewn bench, occasionally pausing to hike up the drooping waistband of her pants. At some point, she'd have to look into picking up a belt. But Shelby could think of any number of things she would rather buy than clothes. Upper most in her mind was a little bite of Bliss.

The dealer didn't show until all the morning buses had come and gone. He strolled over, the soles of his high-tops scraping a steady, rasping tempo, setting her teeth on edge. He didn't seem to notice Shelby as she waited nearby, ringing her hands in anticipation.

He plopped onto the bench as if he owned it and splayed out his long, skinny-jeans clad legs into tripping hazards. With his head bent, his face looked like something ghastly, washed-out by the cool, corpse-blue display of his phone.

"Hey," Shelby murmured as she walked over. She stopped in front of him, blocking the sun from his form, casting him in shade. The guy looked up and started. A confused frown altered the pimple-rimmed foothills around his mouth. He leaned back to take her in.

"I know you…" he proclaimed with an almost musical inflection. "You're that fat girl I sold that B to. Damn…what happened to you?"

Shelby shrugged, not sure how to answer. Besides, she didn't have the time or the desire to chat. Would a guy like him even understand what she'd mean if she said true love?

"Yeah, that was me." The morning sun burned hot on her skin, prickling it angrily. Shelby rubbed the length of tingling flesh as the dealer watched her passively. "Um…hey…" she continued. "I was wondering…do you have any more of that stuff you sold me? I'd like some." At his arched eyebrow, she added a mumbled, "please?"

He sat up, his phone forgotten, and draped an arm along the back of the bench. Instead of looking casual though, the taut line of his long limb gave the ruse away. That and the clenched fist at its end.

"Sorry," he announced with false cheer. "No can do."

"What?" Shelby exclaimed. "Why not?"

"Cause you got the last two I had, chica; hence the deal. Order came down the food-chain to off-load the stuff fast; no more shipments to come in."

"But why?" she repeated, unable to keep the quiver out of her voice.

He shrugged, the movement hampered by the stiff lay of his arm.

"Can't say for sure, but if you put a gun to my head and made me guess, I'd hazard what the news has been sayin' got buyers scared. All those addicts, dropping like flies. Scared buyers means curious cops, and the people who share my unique talent set prefer to stay out of that kind of scrutiny. Only the desperate or the damned seek it out now. Which're you?"

Shelby waved away his comments as if they were flies buzzing round her rooftop. *Think*…she had to think. It was just so hard with the sun's glare slicing daggers of light past her squint, making her eyes water. She wouldn't lose her beloved now, not when they'd only just found each other.

"Look," she said a little too loudly. "If you don't have any on you, I know you know where I can get some more. You have your connections, right? Maybe one of them can help me?"

The guy leaned forward, all semblance of ease forgotten.

"Listen…" he said, pointing a surprisingly well-manicured finger at her. "I know the idea of a dealer with a conscious is…what's the word…ironic? But if a good time is what you're lookin' for, you don't need the Bliss. You and me could hang out sometime…maybe and have ourselves an all-natural high." He punctuated his offer with a little pelvic tilt that showcased his huge belt buckle of a scorpion cast in resin. Shelby took a step back, her shadow dropping away from the planes of his face. The dealer smiled up at her, a cocky thing: all wag and no bark. "But hear me when I tell you…let the Bliss go. It ain't safe; like, I mean, more unsafe than anything else I could sell you. People aren't comin' back from wherever it is their trips take them, and that's bad for business."

He went back to the game on his phone, his side of the conversation obviously over. Shelby looked down at him for a while, let the weight of her stare settle on his crown. His bottle-blond hair shone platinum beneath the unhindered fall light, the careful spikes of his gelled mop as unmoved by her plight as their owner.

"How much?"

The college boy's fingers moved over his phone's display, but other than that motion, she could have been holding a conversation with a department store dummy.

"How much for what?" he asked.

"How much will it cost me for an introduction to whoever you got your Bliss from? Or, if that won't work, to get me as close to the source as you can put me?"

"Girl, you're crazy!" he yelled, glancing up at her. "I just said that stuff will kill you. There's no coming back from dead. No rehab for corpses."

Shelby crossed her arms.

"What do you care?" she asked, spite making her words sharp. "You didn't even know I existed until a couple weeks ago."

The dealer stared at her for a few seconds, his usual self-assured smile replaced by something hard.

"It's more than I'm worth to arrange some kind of meet-and-greet with the higher-ups, but maybe there's someone who can help you. I don't know."

Shelby leaned forward.

"You don't know if they'll help me?" she asked.

"I don't know if she's still alive," he explained, shaking his head. "Look…the name I heard was Tina. Never met her myself, but word is the B bit her bad. Sold her car, her house…everything. Stocked-up on a metric shit-ton of Bliss and rat-holed into the Motel 6 down by the highway. No one's seen her for weeks. If she's still alive, maybe she'd consider selling you some of her spares. If she's dead, well…you might just get 'em for free."

By the time Shelby'd made it the nine or so miles to the motel, she was shaking so bad it was hard to walk straight. Course, the dizziness didn't help. Or the rain, which slicked the road into planes of polished obsidian, needy to glut on skinned knees and gouge into unprotected palms.

Her only companion was the storm whose ashen clouds had swept across the sky with a reckoning to force the day into premature night. Alone, in the full press of that darkness, Shelby imagined her soul was on its last journey, and that soon she'd meet the ferryman waiting for all wanderers on his water-logged craft. Too bad she was without any coins.

Exertion renewed her fever, but at least it'd kept the chill at bay and teased her tired brain into seeing fancies. From the corners of her eyes danced flickers of light, like dozens of tiny candle flames. Fairy lanterns Gran-gran had once called them, her voice growing thick on a mother-tongue Shelby'd never heard before. It'd been a tale of warning, a verbal ward against the threat of the light's false promise.

Her grandparents would be in bed by now or out with the police looking for their missing granddaughter, and their more valuable missing payroll. Shelby waited for the familiar twinge of guilt to sour her already bile-filled stomach. When it didn't come, she was relieved. She'd done what was needed. How else could it have gone?

Her grandfather had never intended to pay her for what she did around the shop, and with all his undocumented workers and their under-the-table wages…well, it was just too easy for her to swipe what money she could and scram. With what she'd scrounged from her "side-job," Shelby hoped it'd be enough to turn Tina's head. It had to be. There was no going back now.

When had she last had something to eat? To drink? Shelby could no longer remember, and it came as something of a relief; one less thing to worry about.

Blisters, which had bloomed across her callused heels, now oozed a sticky, stinging castigation. Shelby welcomed the pain. Her muscle cramps were scourge wounds, her sweat the body-warm blood that pooled in the small of her back. She reveled in her own private penance and sought solace, not in the destination, but in the sacrifice. There was nothing nobler than to burn for love, to waste away the useless housing of flesh if it meant the heart was secure. Love was a woman's holy pilgrimage. There was no higher cause than that.

Eight lights glowed from the windows of the complex, like the drowsy eyes of some giant, maleficent spider. The plan whirled around, disjointed, in her head as Shelby limped along the causeway, past the row of occupied rooms. Each was shut against her except one, it's window cracked open to let in the freezing chill and let out the unmistakable odor of unwashed body and the tang of old urine. A Do Not Disturb sign swayed languidly from the door's tarnished brass handle.

Shelby raised her hand to knock but paused. A sound, like the groan of a wounded animal, murmured at the edges of her perception. It was faint, easy to dismiss. She curled her icy fingers under the window frame, slid it the rest of the way open, and crawled inside.

The room was dim, lit only by the muted sitcom on the television. Shelby glanced around. Whoever this Tina was, she'd been a busy bee. The place looked like it would have been more at home in a hospital than a motel.

An IV stand, top-heavy with empty and half-empty bags, stood like some kind of stainless steel tree bearing sickened fruit. The bedclothes were discolored from what must have been weeks of night-sweats and even darker, more repulsive stains. Packages of adult diapers added silent testimony to the appalling scene, if the stench of their used remains wasn't proof enough.

Shelby gagged and covered her mouth with her sleeve. It smelled like something had died or was soon enough on its way out for the stench to bear enough of a resemblance. All the furniture, except for the bed, had been shoved into one corner of the room. In their place, a row of wooden easels supported upon their spindly frames a series of paintings, each depicting the same elfin-like face of a young woman in a cream-colored dress. Beneath the portraits lay mounds of faded lavender roses, their petals shriveled and browned with decay. The place struck Shelby as a strange conglomeration of cesspit and shrine.

She tip-toed toward the closed bathroom door, careful to sidestep the piles of mysterious medical waste which littered the carpet. The moaning was louder here, definitely coming from inside the room.

"Hello?" Shelby called out. "Tina?"

"Yes!" a woman's weak voice answered. "I'm in here. Oh dear God, please help me."

Shelby pushed the door open slowly. The lights were off in this room too, but she could clearly hear the ragged panting of someone on the floor.

"I need to turn on the lights," Shelby explained as she reached over and flipped the switch.

"No wait—" Tina began, but her words trailed off into a startled shriek as the fluorescents above the sink flared to life.

Shelby stared down at the nude woman sprawled at her feet. She didn't know who she'd been expecting to meet by coming here, but somebody's mother or grandmother hadn't been it.

The older woman was pale, or had been before whatever sickness she now suffered from had tinted her skin yellow. What wasn't jaundiced was swollen red and angry, and a smell, not unlike rotting meat, assaulted Shelby's nostrils. Layers of wrinkled flesh puddled over the stark xylophone of the woman's ribs and down to the false waistband of what could only be a severe case of diaper rash.

Tina's arm, more bone than flesh, clawed at a nearby wash rag. She splayed it across one of her breasts in an attempt at modesty. The other breast lay flat, deflated, against the bony housing of her chest.

"What happened to you?" Shelby asked, unable to hide her grimace.

How could someone come to this, be reduced to such a state? Shelby forced her eyes to stay fixed on the sharp, skeletal planes of the cringing woman's face and not stray to the decay of the rest of her body.

Tina sucked in a breath between clenched teeth. "I slipped when I was trying to get into the tub," she explained, voice coming out in a whispered rasp. "I think I've broken a few ribs, maybe fractured my hip." She had an arm tucked in tight against her side, and what wasn't concealed by that pathetic wing was purpled by a large bruise. At Shelby's continued stare, she fell quiet. "Wait a minute," Tina said, shaking her head. "You're not with the staff."

Shelby tried to swallow past the sand pit in her mouth but couldn't scrounge up the spit with which to do it.

"Who are you?" Tina asked, clasping the wash rag tighter to her chest. "What are you doing in my room?"

"I'm—" Shelby began.

"No wait," she interrupted, squinting up at her. "Don't tell me. I can see it heavy on you, girl."

"See what?"

Tina's chuckle turned into a hiss of pain. "Can't hide what you are, child. Not from one of your own. So…you've been bit too. What's that got to do with you being here?"

Shelby sighed and took a knee. The cold, ceramic tile made for a painful perch. How Tina had suffered on it for the hours she must have been there, Shelby couldn't say.

"I came here to buy some B," she admitted.

Tina snorted. "That's rich. Whoever heard of a junkie sharing their stash? Addicts aren't known for their generosity. Anyway, even if I had extra, I wouldn't give you any."

"Why not?"

"Are you blind, girl? You don't want to end up like me. Besides, I'm all out."

Tina shifted her arm away from her bruise. On its underside were dozens of pale scars, like dash marks, crisscrossing Tina's skin into a fractal of wounds. Two Bliss patches, one flaking and used, the other still new, stretched plastered amid the organized mutilation of flesh.

"That's my last," Tina explained, tilting her arm out so Shelby could see. "But I've got to get cleaned up first. You see…she doesn't want me because I'm filthy and sick. But this is what she's going to get," she growled. "She made me into this, goddammit, so she'll take me whether she likes it or not!" Drained by the outburst, Tina lay back onto the icy tiles and stared up at the ceiling. "It wasn't always like this, you know. We were seventeen when we met. Our families were both vacationing at the same resort. When I first saw her, it felt like my heart stopped. She was so beautiful."

Shelby nodded, though the older woman couldn't have seen the gesture.

"We spent those long summer nights together on the beach," Tina went on, "but then autumn came, and we had to leave. We promised to be pen-pals, and I wrote to her every week for twenty years until she died. She was the love of my life; my husband and kids couldn't understand my grief. But then she came back to me. And she was just as beautiful, just as young and full of life as the moment we met. And she'll stay with me to the end; she owes me that." Tina turned her head and gazed at a small container balanced on the lip of the bathtub. "Just as soon as I get the strength up for one last visit."

Shelby followed her stare to the prescription bottle. "What's that for?"

"To make sure one more visit is all I'll have. This body is done; I've worn it out. But I've had a helluva run. Early on, I figured out how to keep our little dance going, to keep the music playing. I used my skills as a nurse to keep me nourished when I was down, and medicated when I came back. I've drawn the courtship out for months now, but I'm tired of the run-around, and so is she. She wants her fill of what I have left to give, and I don't have the fight in me to draw it out any longer." Tina stared down the length of her withered body at Shelby. "But you didn't come here for a chat, did you?"

Shelby shook her head slowly.

"And you haven't exactly jumped up and offered to help me, have you?"

"No, I haven't."

"It's useless kid; this hard line you're walking. I don't have any more B."

Shelby stood and stared down at Tina. The thing beneath her was damaged and weak, undeserving.

"Yes, you do," she stated coldly.

"Search the room if you don't believe me!" Tina ordered with a harsh whisper. "Just help me into that tub before you go. For god's sake, send me off in peace!"

Shelby leaned over Tina and grabbed her arm. The older woman struggled, but there wasn't enough fight left in her to keep Shelby from ripping the fresh bite of Bliss from her arm. Tina snarled up at Shelby like an old dog: teeth bared, but the threat hollow.

"No!" she wailed, as Shelby straightened back up. "You can't take my last one! I need it! I need to see her one more time!"

Shelby glanced over at the prescription bottle before swiping it up too. Tina had seemed to think that the pills would make for a longer date, a deeper connection. Stepping back, Shelby retreated to the bathroom doorway. She cast one last look at Tina.

"Don't worry," she said, tossing a bath towel at the older woman to give her something to cover herself with. "Someone will find you tomorrow."

As Shelby pulled the bathroom door shut on Tina's garbled cries, she glanced down at the woad-blue B in her hand. The sigil shone eerily bright in the dim room like a brand across her palm. Or a favor.

Shelby unmuted the television set as she passed. The laugh track from the sitcom drowned out the noise that came from the bathroom, melding Tina's ghostly wails into the loops of canned mirth. Shelby paused at the door to flip the Do Not Disturb sign over. Let the cleaning crew find Tina on their morning rounds; by then Shelby'd be long gone.

The little bottle of pills jangled a rattling tempo from Shelby's pocket as she darted through the parking lot and across the street. The rain had not let up during her time in the motel room and now poured down upon her like blood from a hemorrhaged wound. Across the way, the relative safety of a secluded green-space promised both privacy and a chance to get dry.

She surged forward, heart pounding in her chest. She'd done it! She couldn't believe she'd actually done it. She'd proven herself for her love, and now they could be together. Forever.

Shelby clutched the tiny patch of plastic in her hand, eager to experience its bite once more. The need to slip into that secret realm and feel the kiss of her lover all but consumed her. If she didn't get there soon, Shelby was sure she'd die of desire.

The lights, which had before danced at her periphery, now soared across the landscape of her sight, thrumming against the night like electricity along an exposed nerve end. The chaos was dazzling, a painful, pretty kaleidoscope, which hummed a toneless tune that called to Shelby, urging her onward. Her body burned as if on fire, a lighthouse to guide Him to her.

Darkness swallowed her stumbling form as swaths of salal bushes and blackberry vines scraped and tore into her skin in a greedy demand for tribute. It was black here, like the first long night of the universe, and soon Shelby no longer knew where she was or where she was going.

But that didn't matter. The only thing that was important was her lover and her need to be with Him while the night could still bear its kind face to what they would share. All too soon, morning would come and ruin the dream…but maybe it didn't have to.

Forward. That was the only thought in her fevered mind. That and soon; soon she would see Him.

Had she walked miles from the motel? Tens of miles? The smells were deeper here, loamy, and heavy with the scent of decay and cold, stagnant water. The fairy lanterns which had once guided her were all but gone, their tiny caretakers perhaps tiring of their malicious game.

She found herself in some kind of clearing at the top of a knoll. At its center sprawled what looked to be a large metal carcass, like some prehistoric creature left to rot in the wild. The exposed hollow, where the massive aluminum beast had been felled by a gash to its side, yawned invitingly to its wayward traveler.

Shelby climbed inside the corpse, surprised to find it filled with the shades of furniture. On hands and knees, she inched through the mildewed innards toward the rear of the beast and collapsed onto the soggy mattress she found there.

A shard of jutting metal served as her razor. With shaky hands, Shelby cut a deep furrow across the plains of her forearm's flesh. The Bliss came next. The plastic brand smeared against the puddle of her blood before finally adhering to the edges of her laceration. Last came the bottle of pills, which Shelby upended into her mouth, her dry throat struggling with the bitter tablets.

The discs clung to her tongue, tenacious. She didn't have enough spit in her mouth to make them go down. The world tilted. The sour tang of bile tickled at the back of her throat. Shelby lay atop the wet mattress, her limbs too weak to move her. Water…she needed water, something to get the things down with!

Raindrops echoed atop the enclosed ribcage of the metal monster she lay within, their waters tantalizingly close yet still out of reach. The warmth was fading from her body, the lure of sleep like an anchor pulling her down. But she had to get those pills swallowed so she could be with Him longer. So she could stay.

With a desperate thirst, Shelby clamped down onto the open wound of her arm and suckled at the fluid she found there, drawing it down, letting the coppery syrup fill her mouth and ease the pills' passage.

She closed her eyes, her quickly cooling blood a shushing palm print across her mouth. The sound of the rain was like some ancient lullaby, soothing her into sleep. Her shaking stopped. She was no longer cold. She wasn't afraid…

He was waiting for her when she awoke.

This time, though, he was different. This time he wasn't human.

Black, hairless skin formed the casing of his body. Its leathery folds cascaded into elongated flaps which connected his arms to his sides. His face, once so handsome, was still striking, but the elements were strange, bestial. His nose truncated into something like a snout, perched high above a thin-lipped mouth drawn back to reveal a pair of pink-tinged fangs. Only his eyes were the same, as brilliant and hungry as ever.

"You've come," he said slowly, his teeth making the words lisp a little. "I did not know if you would."

"Of course I did," Shelby admitted in a small voice. "I love you."

Her voice was her own, and when she glanced down, Shelby saw that though she was naked, her body was the same old thing she wore when she was awake.

He nodded as if graciously accepting a compliment. "And how do you find me?" he asked, arching his arms out behind him to form a cape of the thin, veined membrane of his wings. "Still pleasing to look upon?"

His words were edged, daring Shelby to impale herself upon them with a careless lie. She shrugged, not sure what to say.

"I don't know," she explained, worry snaking into her words to make them sound hollow and childlike. "Has *everything* about you changed?"

"No," he admitted, voice softening. "I am still me…underneath."

Shelby stared at him. Though he looked different, for some reason there was still something about him that bound her to him. Even in the face of his revelation, she wasn't afraid. Or repulsed. Only the prettiest creatures could hide such horrors within.

"So am I," she admitted with a whisper, hating the truth of it. How long had she hoped her own body could be like his was now, a shell concealing something pure within? Her own ugliness seeped from the inside out, like a festered wound that needed to be lanced.

"And do you truly love me," he asked, voice gentle, "now that you know what I really am?"

The question seemed rude but had to be asked. "What are you, really?"

"I am a parasite," he explained, drawing his lips back to accent his fangs. He hissed the word, stretching it out until it turned sibilant.

"Then what am I?" she asked, tears threatening the question.

He strode forward. His taloned feet clicked across the floor with each step as if a host of scorpions scurrying away at his approach.

When just a few feet separated them, he reached out a clawed hand and ran the back of his fingers slowly down the length of her cheek.

"You are mine," he explained, his coal-dark eyes burning into hers. Shelby stared into them and saw the familiar conglomeration of her features mirrored there. She felt Him too, inside her, as much a part of herself as she was.

Tears fell heedless down her cheeks and lapped against the Stygian shores of his fingers.

"Are you going to kill me?" An image of Tina, lying broken on the bathroom floor as she waited for her chance to die, came to mind.

He moved forward, swallowing up the distance between them. His hand drew up and across her temple, his fingers splaying possessively into the territory of her hair.

"Do you want me to?"

"Yes," she heard herself admit. As soon as the word was spoken, she knew it was true. Shelby couldn't stand the thought of going back. Not to that life. Not to a place where she would once again be meaningless and unloved.

"Why?" he asked, the question soft and warm against her cheek. "I could let you go, you know. There is still some time, if you hurried."

Shelby tilted her head to press into his touch. "I wasn't alive until you found me. Why would I want to go back to that?"

"Because this is not real," he explained slowly, as if speaking to a small child. "It never was. It was all just stage-dressing and costumes, pure fantasy."

Shelby shook her head slightly. "You're wrong. It was more real to me than anything I've ever felt."

He smiled or something close to it. "So, even now, you think it was love?"

She almost blurted out yes. Wasn't that why she'd done it, done everything? But no, as she thought back, maybe it wasn't love, not entirely. It was something deeper, something truer, which had made her continue to go to him. Something selfless and pure and just as consuming.

"You needed me," she stated simply. "All of me. That was how I fell in love with you. The fantasy was just a dream, a game we played to convince us it wasn't one-sided. But I don't care if it was, or if it still is...I just wanted to matter to someone. More than love, you gave me life, a reason for existing. You gave me hope, which... maybe...is even stronger than love. I wanted to be someone's entire world, and, for a while, I was."

"But you are dying, and I led you to it. What does that say about this world of yours?"

"I don't know. But, it doesn't matter, because I know you had to. It's your nature."

He was silent for a few moments, the tips of his clawed fingers swirled gently across her scalp. He drew his hand away and placed it across her chest. The inky flesh was clammy but warm on her breast.

With delicate care, he pressed two fingers into the skin there, puncturing the flesh with a pair of tiny pinpricks. Shelby flinched but did not move away, the pain a welcome thing as long as it was accompanied by his soft touch.

"You are very young..." he continued, withdrawing his hand. With a deft movement, he drew a claw across the puckered line of his lips, splitting them open to allow a kind of green ichor to emerge. "...and I am very old."

Leaning forward, he pressed his wounded mouth to Shelby's breast. He kissed her there, his blood allowing the motion to slicken across her chest, painting her with a palette of gore. A cascade of quickening pleasure found her, rioting spasm after spasm of pure sensation through her womb. Within the span of two heartbeats, her universe exploded in a boundless macrocosm of immeasurable delight.

But it was too much. Almost too much. Shelby clutched at him, afraid to let go.

All too soon, he pulled away.

He stared at her, the folds of his lips knitting together and mending before her eyes. His blood remained, however, and made his face waxy with its wet veneer.

"Through this kiss I swear to you, my beloved," he proclaimed, his bloodied lips curling into a smile, "you will never be alone again."

* * *

That night, Shelby was a starlet, a silicone-filled creature that could have stepped right off a magazine cover. Only her engorged breasts broke the polite illusion of this exaggeration of reality. That, and her bottle-tanned skin.

The prospect approached, crowned with a swath of platinum hair spiked into a punk-rocker's do. His pale skin gleamed in the candlelit twilight, as did the near-invisible embossed "B" etched upon his flesh.

Somewhere nearby, her dark lover awaited and watched with an ancient care these first few steps Shelby took in her new life. She could feel his graceful insistence, the quiet pride her continued success brought Him. But more than anything, she could feel his need.

They were both hungry this night.

"Who are you?" the prospect asked, voice low and sultry. Even with the overly masculine affectation, the unmistakable stress of a European diction crept around the corners of his question.

Shelby strode forward, the petite gait of her delicate form still something to get used to, and dispelled the distance between them.

"I am yours," she proclaimed, baptizing the promise with a hungry kiss.

XOXOX XOXOX XOXOX X

About the Author

From the whimsical to the macabre, S.B. Roark's genre-crossing works appear in anthologies like *Witches, Stitches & Bitches, Give: An Anthology of Anatomical Entries, Melt: Five Stories to Get Snowed in With,* and more. Along with writing, S.B. edits for small presses and brought to light *Rachel* by Dobromir Harrison that later appeared on John Scalzi's blog. S.B. frequents local science fiction and fantasy conventions as the occasional panelist, critiques for the writing workshops, and is the Managing Editor for SinCyr Publishing. As secretary of Cascade Writers, a nonprofit writing workshop, S.B. assists in bringing community, creativity, and contacts to authors at every level of career development.

Rock Bottom

Nick Barton

1.
You Have Been Here Before

Adistant car horn cuts across the silence. You wait for the sound of squealing tires announcing another hit and run, but no sound comes. Dwarfed by the concrete canyon, you walk alone, facing the snow blowing in the wind. The cold bites your face, as if winter has a grudge against you. Subway smoke billows through the grates as trains hurtle underground. A discarded sandwich board lies on the pavement, its message faded beyond legibility. Another hope for another life lost to the ages, but this doesn't surprise you.

You are at Rock Bottom. The end of the world as you know it, and there is no greater punishment. But there is an upside.

The only way is up.

It's been two years since your arrival, and the place has welcomed you like a long lost son. The streetlights know your name. They cast your shadow tall and wide across the immortal night. Dead memories flutter through the atmosphere like rubbish caught in the wind. Sometimes you catch the ghosts of voices in the air, their words unknown.

Reaching the intersection, devoid of traffic, you see the skyscraper. LONELY TOWER gleams in white across the middle. Nobody shadows the bright windows, but you know they are there. Clad in black, they are always there. Watching. Waiting.

A car rounds the corner. You back off, giving the driver room to correct their approach. Bucking on the curb, it hobbles back on the asphalt. It swerves slowly as if following a phantom slalom. As it passes, you peer in to take a look. Slumped to the side, the woman turns the wheel with one hand, the other unseen. Careering from lane to lane, she goes on, becoming a dot, then twin taillights, and then nothing.

You cross the road for the skyscraper. Dreading every moment.

Inside the Lonely Tower, you brush snow off your shoulders. Calm music would pervade Topside buildings, but Rock Bottom melodies play a miserable cadence like funeral ambience.

You approach the receptionist, Agent Plath. A cigarette dangles off her lip, the red cherry a bright spot of color in the monochromatic lobby. Her eyes are dead lights of apathy.

"Appointment?"

You give your name and time. She types without urgency. Why would she? It's 2:58 a.m. The Lonely Hour. The world has stopped turning.

"Agent Churchill is on the top floor."

She doesn't need to tell you this. You have been here before.

The doors glide open to 104. Giant windows present the dark skyline. Standing close enough to steam the glass with your breath, you observe the sprawling labyrinth below. You search for the drunk driver, but there are no drifting lights down there. Just streetlights winking your name.

Two others sit in the waiting room. One is reading a magazine, and another studies empty Chinese takeaway boxes scattered by his feet. One reason binds you all here. It's shining through a glass ceiling, towering through the dark clouds.

A man tugs your arm. It's Takeaway China.

You see where he's pointing. Tall, top hat, and stern eyes, the Agent of Despair beckons you to his office. Churchill is written on his door.

Churchill closes the door as you sit opposite his desk. He sits down with a grunt and flicks through his pile of paper-clipped documents. The fax machine beeps, and he snatches a page from its jaws. He takes his stamp in the dish of red ink and leaves it there like a judge's gavel. Eager to use.

You, and everybody else, loathe the Agents of Despair. Overseeing the streets from their ivory tower, they decide who stays and who goes. It's a simple test, and you have failed every time. Misery deepens inside your heart, well aware what shade Churchill will color his stamp.

"Give me a reason why I should stamp this green." The ghost of a leader lingers behind his stern, bored voice. Only now, it's more apt of turning unities into mutinies.

Reconciliation is seldom found in their hearts, but you swallow your bad mood and petition for escape. After all, you have earned it.

"I followed the rules," you say. A flicker of the lips, a hoisting eyebrow. Churchill is indifferent. Soulless. "I have a home, a job, a good wage. Three basics for Rock Bottom life. I have done my time."

It's a short speech, hardly a speech at all, but it wears you out. Churchill hasn't changed. His fingers reach for the stamp.

REJECTED.

You leave like always. Emotionless outside, crying like hell inside.

Agent Plath books your next appointment in six months. You take the card to update your diary with the time and date. And the disappointment.

Back outside, you spot an Agent of Despair walking alone, weak snow swirling around him like a shroud. He looks at you. Cold, dark eyes. Red beard lifting with a sneer. Van Gogh. Another keeper of lost souls, just like Plath and Churchill.

The weak lights of Unhappy Hour beckon you closer.

Misery loves company.

2.
UNHAPPY HOUR

Heartbreak rock haunts Unhappy Hour's heartbroken atmosphere. Words come and go like the tide's approach and retreat. You watch the foam atop your pint glass dissolve. Every sip is like a sea of sorrow crashing against your teeth. It might be weak, but it's still beer, and you could do with winding down.

Glancing around the bar, everybody fosters the same look of indifference that is so common, it's almost as if everybody has forgotten how to smile. Topside funerals have more character than this. It's something in the air; you are sure of it. You think about the Lonely Tower. That spire isn't a lift ascending above the clouds, but a chimney pumping out misery like smoke.

Headlights sweep past the window. It might be the drunk woman, but your mind is in recovery mode from Churchill's refusal. During the Lonely Hour, there isn't much call for interest outside your own life.

The barman slings a dishtowel over his shoulder and slides another glass across the table. A man wearing a suit and trilby catches it. A quarter of the pint is gone. Taking the bait, you too take a swig, then clench in panic. You heave over and cough your lungs out, pounding your chest like a man struck by an arrhythmia. The barman teeters on the cusp of laughter.

"Oh, you do make an old man happy."

You sink another mouthful and slam your glass down, as if to prove a point. The barman has already moved on. The ashtrays need emptying. Normality's returned, or is it just your heart rate that's returned to normal? The music goes on, depressing songs preluding the end of hope.

"How is Churchill these days?"

The man at the edge is looking at his glass, examining the suds inside. You look around. You can't be sure it was him who spoke, but everybody else — all six behind you — are busy studying their own drinks, trying to work out when everything fell apart.

He waves at you. "Hello?"

Now you glare at him.

"How is Churchill?"

No words come to mind.

The man sighs. "It isn't a difficult question. I know you see him."

"He's fine," you answer.

"He shouldn't be," the man says. He leans toward you as if hustling product across the bar. Your eyes drift to his trilby. The brim looks sharp enough to cut down a tree, and you wonder what's hidden inside. Cigarettes, perhaps? "Would you like to know how many people he has cleared Topside?"

You shrug, not looking at him.

"One."

"One?"

He nods, tapping his fingers against the glass. His eyes are on the barman rummaging around in the back. "I know his name, you know."

"I'm sorry, why are you telling me this?"

"Because you want to leave Rock Bottom, yes?"

"Of course I do."

"And Churchill is your agent?"

You nod, growing impatient with these cryptic messages.

He turns to face you, bright eyes shining beneath the brim of his trilby. "Then I'm sorry. He won't clear you."

You look at the foamy sea in your glass. The thought of another drink is more depressing than returning to your flat. You've already slung out a rat last week. Sometimes it sounds like they're scuttling inside the walls and beneath the floorboards.

Saying goodbye, you leave the stranger to his drink and open the door. A gust of wind roars inside, spraying snow.

The barman flaps his dishcloth. "Whoa, close the door!"

You are already gone.

Jagged cracks in the pavement mark your way home. Impulses to dart inside an alley and cry shout like voices in your head. You can feel the eyes of the Lonely Tower watching you, wondering if you'll turn your life around or sink deeper into darkness.

You unlock your flat. It's not as gloomy as you thought. It's worse. The bed is unmade, spilling over the edge as if you fell out of bed. Dirty dishes resemble shipwrecks in the sink. Footprints mark where you've trodden on the dusty carpet, and dust colonizes each surface. Some items remain as mementos of Topside life, but their memories fade every day, like photographs left in the light. Their faces becoming mannequins, soon to become ghosts.

You notice the bathroom light is on. Puzzling. You remember switching it off. Moving to the door, you freeze.

The man with the trilby is flossing in the mirror.

"Hello."

3.
THE MAN OF HOPE

Bolts of jealousy stab your chest. This is a man at home, quietly tending to his dental needs, and it's *you* who feels like an intruder. Questions race across your mind like motorway traffic, but you remain quiet, keen on what he has to say.

He grins a toothy smile at the mirror, checking his handiwork before looping the thread of floss and dropping it in the bin.

"Had to bring my own," he says, brushing his brow.

"Sorry to ruin your day," you tell him.

He stands straight, tugging his suit as if adjusting his appearance before a night out. "No need to apologize, you—"

"What do you want?"

He doesn't turn around, still captivated by his own reflection. In a way, you are glad. Who knows what lurks inside the eyes of a man who can beat you home this fast? And there is the question of security to consider. The keys in your hand remind you there are no spares.

"You left before I could finish my story," he answers.

"I thought you had finished."

"Not quite." He raises his chin, checking for rogue hairs, you suspect. Needless, since he has the shiniest jawline you have ever seen.

Impatient, you turn for the living room/bedroom/kitchen and slump on the couch. You remember your initial reaction when you first stepped foot inside this matchbox. A bottomed mood sank into the seabed. Any hope of making this place your own was quickly dashed away by an unmovable page of wallpaper above the TV and the rat hole. No matter how hard you pulled, it wouldn't budge. Walls painted slate, it made that solitary page even more infuriating.

The rats would then come out to scavenge the leftovers, disturbing your depression.

On TV, the news recounts the day. It's the same every day on every channel. News reporters discussing the plague of apathy.

"It's rude to leave your guest."

You look at him by the doorway, dusting his hands.

"You're an intruder, not a guest."

He tips his hat like he's greeting an acquaintance.

"True. Would you like me to leave, or do you want to hear the rest of my story?"

Temptation tugs at your sleeve. You want him gone, but life in Rock Bottom hasn't dulled your senses. He followed you for a reason.

Taking your silence as confirmation to stay, he sits on the footrest abandoned by the bookshelf.

"I was going to tell you I can help you pass your test."

You are about to tell him fairy tales don't exist, but his eyes glimmer a starry sky you haven't seen since Topside. You lower your guard but mindful sentries stand watch, ready for disappointment.

"Can you prove it to me?"

He slips his hand inside his jacket, never breaking eye contact. He presents a quartered sheet of paper. As if handling noxious goods, you pick the page with your thumb and forefinger. Encouraged by a nod, you unfold it. Your heart skips a beat.

ACCEPTED.

The letters stamped green appear off-world, like it's an impossible color. How would you feel to unfold your own acceptance letter? Insomnia had mothered hallucinations, and sometimes you saw REJECTED blink on the alarm clock instead of the time. Churchill's pudgy face haunts your mind in and out of sleep, and when you do drift off, Topside memories pass by like lonely clouds riding a clear sky. You are no codebreaker, but you search for clues in the letter. No, it's impossible. How could you convince Churchill of your happiness? He goes through red ink like Unhappy Hour goes through whisky.

This time you read the bottom line.
Signed,
Churchill.

"I was his first," the man says. "The appointment went on for five hours. People waiting were either flogged to another agent or rescheduled. Churchill was certain I was lying."

"How did you convince him?" Desperation sounds in your voice. You try to look in control, but let's be honest, when were you last in control?

"Repetition," he says. Catching your raised brow, he goes on. "I mean it. Stick to your mood, and he'll believe it. Eventually. I told him I was happy over and over and *over* again. When he checked my mood reports from work, he got angry. He called the factory, and the manager confirmed their accuracy. High mood levels, no suicidal signs or irritation spikes. Level like a plain."

The sheet wilts in your hand. He takes it back, refolding it.

Your head wanders back to the Lonely Tower. Its spire poking through the clouds like a periscope, probing the place you can't reach. Topside. Full of color, life, and second chances. On your descent into Rock Bottom, you saw the reasons behind your exile play out like a credits list. Her face was there, pale and beautiful, as was the car, and the shriek of a baby.

"When was this?" You point at his jacket, where he has the letter.

"Two years ago."

Your mouth falls open, half-expecting your tongue to follow like a rolling carpet.

"Then why are you still here?"

His smile is brighter than the streetlights.

"To help you reach Topside."

This is a trick. You are sure of it. There is no way out of Rock Bottom. The Agents of Despair hold the keys, and they never unlock the doors.

You stand up and lean by the window, watching the streetlights wink your name in their silent language. A distant car horn blares. The drunk woman still running free.

"I was like you once," the man says. "I know what it's like. This place makes you worse and worse, and every rejection sends you to the bar. I lived here, too."

You say nothing, eyes on the still road.

"I'll bet you've hidden your rejection slips somewhere. Stuffed in a pillowcase or kept in a bathroom cabinet?"

Your eyes flick to the rat hole. A lock loosens inside you, the chain rattling to break free. You face him and see a man in deep recall, his eyes focused on nothing.

"Why would you think—?"

"I even had a similar haircut, but mine was going at the sides." He gestures at your feet. "I had black shoes as well. Mine were scuffed worse than yours."

You sit down, afraid your legs will give out.

"I had the same scruff on my chin as well, but as you can see," he raises his head like a poster-boy, proclaiming victory, "I cleaned up my act. Partly why I earned my green stamp."

Desert winds had dried your mouth. Now a fresh spring waters your tongue enough to ask for his name.

"You can call me Hope."

4.
GHOSTS

The man who calls himself Hope stays quiet, waiting for you to talk. Thoughts clash together. Ghosts have never come up in your mind, but you are questioning your own belief now. The truth appears to be sitting before you, smiling warmly with a trilby propped on his head, and a jawline so clean, it looks like it has never met a razor.

I even had a similar haircut, but mine was going at the sides.

You gesture at his hat. "T-take it off."

He bows a little and slips off his hat, holding it upside down like a busker asking for tips. His dome, shiny like his jawline, and his sides are indeed grey.

"Are you really…?"

Hope flips his hat back on. "I was accepted shortly before you arrived."

Your eyes drift to the peeling page of wallpaper. When the nights are warm enough to warrant an open window, you can hear the page flapping in the draft.

"I used sticky tape." He gestures at the wallpaper.

"I've tried that," you answer. "It just falls off."

Hope passes his hand down his face, staring at the wall. "I was afraid something like that might happen. When flats become vacant, the agents fortify them to resist whatever the last tenant did. I used tape to stop that blasted thing flapping in the breeze. Now it won't work."

You can feel a piece of your mood plummeting like rock falling off a cliff-face, splashing into the crashing waves. You take a deep breath, ignore the wallpaper, and look at the sofa, picking at the patchy leather.

"So, if I leave, the next person won't be able to stuff the rat hole?"

"Not with what you used, no."

You move to the hole, reach inside and pull out a wad of crumpled paper. A squeak comes from inside. A pink nose pokes out, whiskers fluttering. Hesitating, it darts back inside.

Hope gestures at your hand. "Your rejection slips?"

"All of them."

"There was never a rat hole when I lived here."

The sheets fall around your feet like dead leaves. "I hate this place."

Hope leads you to the sofa and sits beside you. "You won't be here for much longer."

His words glance off you like hail against glass. You have seen the acceptance form, and yet you still can't fathom Churchill stamping green. It's a dream you've dreamt for so long you can remember it vividly, but it always comes apart like wet paper. Churchill stamps red every time, and each time, your mood sinks deeper into that sea of sorrow you can't sail. Now you can feel the reef scraping a pattern across the ship's belly. The sails are burning, and you will sink into the seabed, never to be rescued.

"How can you be so sure?" you ask him.

"I have the proof." He taps his breast pocket.

"But I'm not you." You cast your arms around the flat, encouraging a study of your feeble belongings. "I have everything agents want from us, and I still can't leave."

He shakes his head a little too patronizingly for your taste. "You are not happy. Or if you are, then you don't believe it."

"I never said I was happy."

Hope raises his hands with biblical intensity. "Well, there you are. That's why Churchill doesn't clear you."

"How am I supposed to be happy?" More rock slips off the cliff. "How can anyone be happy here?"

Instead of retreating, Hope faces the gauntlet head on. "Repetition."

Breath escapes your lips. You feel underwhelmed, as if waiting for the greatest firework to explode.

"Seriously?"

"Keep doing what you are doing. Keep going to work. Keep waking up, going to bed early, eating right, cutting down on vices. Keep telling yourself where you want to be."

"I've been doing that."

"I know," he says. "I've watched you for two years. But you let the atmosphere take you down. After seeing Churchill, you go to Unhappy Hour. In fact, you go there most nights. You have trouble sleeping—"

"It's the gas they pump out!"

He cocks his head with a patronizing smile, and you want to slam your fist into it.

"You don't still believe that, do you?"

A powerful sigh exhausts all resolve to reply.

"Agents of Despair don't pump out gas. Misery loves nighttime. You must have felt it Topside as well."

As if wiping away condensation from a windowpane, you see the truth. Misery does love the night, and Topside nights were lonelier than these. Echoes of baby mobiles haunted your dreams, and when insomnia held sleep hostage, you thought about the changes brought about by disaster. The double bed was too big for you, the street seemed to scream a void emptiness, and two people were still missing. Never to return.

You look at your lap, knotting your fingers. "It's impossible to be happy here."

"But it is possible to *believe*," Hope says.

"I don't know."

He looks around the flat, taking it all in like a Topside estate agent scouting for selling points. You feel exposed, as if there is a great secret yet to be discovered.

"You've made a good start here."

"What do you mean?"

He stands and takes a book from the counter. Patting dust off the cover, he inspects it. "*Harry Potter and the Philosopher's Stone*? I remember reading this to my son."

"You have a son?"

"Don't be too surprised."

"No, I mean," you sit up, feeling your back groan, "I know nothing about you."

"Topside memories slowly come back with an acceptance letter."

Deflected off-topic, you follow his redirection, promising yourself to question his past another time. "Don't they fade anymore?"

He rocks his hand from side to side. "They come and go, but mostly—" He looks at the book again. "Why is this here?"

You don't want to answer. Talking hurts.

"Don't keep it to yourself," he says. "That's the first step. Talk. Open up."

"I was going to save it for when my daughter turned six."

"Oh."

"Yeah."

He places the book back on the counter, as if it's laced with a lethal pathogen. "You have a daughter?"

"*Had*," you say.

"And is this her?" He moves to a desktop photograph frame on the end of the counter. A wedding ring beside it.

"Yes. And my wife."

He looks at the photo, but you can't bear to. It's one of the few Topside memories that retain their features, coming alive when sleep is out of reach. You are standing beside your wife, arms linked, and the snow glows in the light. Your daughter is waddling in the snow at your feet, captivated by this brand new canvas.

"I think I can guess the next part," Hope says.

You glare at him like a man interrupted from his bereavement. "You don't know anything."

"You are right. I shouldn't pry." He replaces the frame. "At some point, you'll have to face the truth."

You massage your temples. War drums pound the end of the world inside your head, and you debate whether or not to throw him out. "What does that mean?"

"There's a reason why you are here. The sooner you accept what happened, the happier you will be."

The cliff collapses. Anger is set free.

"How can that make me happy?"

"It's a big step," he answers. "You need to accept what happened so you can move on. I had to do it."

"I don't want to think about it."

"You have to."

The TV remote smashes against the wall. Two batteries spin out of sight. Hope doesn't react.

"I said I don't want to talk about it."

In the following quiet, Hope sits beside you. You want to move away, but most of all, you want to sleep. Or at least try.

"In time," he says. "In time it will be easier. You have to believe me."

You bury your head in your hands. "I want to go to bed."

"Okay. I'll wait in the lobby." He hesitates by the door. "Think about what I said. *Really* think about it. Tomorrow is a new day. Goodnight."

The door closes, and you feel the absence of company. How long has it been since someone visited you? Despite what Hope pitched, you miss him. Without anyone to talk to, loneliness returns, harping mad calls.

You raise your head and catch sight of the photo. Tears threaten to break, but you hold them back.

Tonight, you will not cry.

5.
HOWLING

You awake to the alarm clock's maniacal wail.

Washed and ready, you catch something in the mirror. Who is this stranger? It's like a sullen portrait breaking character. Color floods his eyes, the bags are gone, and there is a revived sparkle. Like Hope checking his teeth in the mirror, you flash a toothy grin. Years of coffee have stained them yellow, but who cares? This is who you are now. Smile reborn, reflection adored.

You fetch a tie from the wardrobe. Light blue. A calming color. Top button done, you smile again. You feel ready for work.

In the lobby, Hope stands to greet you. Clad in yesterday's clothes, his grin retains the sunshine warmth devoid in Rock Bottom.

"Good lord." He gestures at his own eyes. "Have you checked baggage claim?"

Smiling hurts your mouth. You clamp a hand against it as if ashamed of what you have done. Hope laughs, but inside you are laughing too.

He swings for the doors. "Let's go to work."

"How do you know where I—?"

Then you remember. He's been following you for two years. At the thought of that, you feel unguarded. This man, this *ghost*, has seen you at your worst. He's watched you drag your failings and disappointments around like a ball and chain. He's seen you sink beer after beer at Unhappy Hour. He's seen you cry on the sofa, watched your tears spot the photo of your wife and daughter like rainfall. He's seen your futile attempts to rip off the wallpaper page, knowing he's the reason why you can't get rid of it. He's seen you try to end your life in the subway station when a patrolman yanked you back, wagged his finger, and returned you to the Lonely Tower. He has seen it all, and yet he believes he can save you.

"Hey?" he says.

You stop on the pavement. Pedestrians weave around you. Is it you or has Rock Bottom changed a little? Something feels different. It's still familiar, but the chronic misery you have become so used to seems to have disappeared. You glance at Hope. He's smiling.

"What do you see?" he asks.

"I see…I see hope."

Another sunshine smile. "I knew something had changed." He gestures to his eyes again. "You slept well, didn't you? No dreams?"

Now that you think about it, sleep had been pleasant. Now you feel recharged and ready to ride the miserable day into the black sunset.

You raise your head like an orphan fearful of following a stranger home. "What's happening to me?"

Hope touches your elbow. "You are beginning to believe."

If this is recovery, then it makes work's usual grind easier to bear. You work to the soundtrack of tapping keys, creating a monotonous melody. You stop for a moment to listen. Gunfire bursts of *tap-tap-tap* break the quiet, followed by more. Some people sigh, others grunt, but one is crying. A Weeper. Most people in Rock Bottom cope with the despair, but Weepers are hopeless cases. Unable or unwilling to recover, they cry until they can't cry anymore. It's rumored Agents of Despair come for them, but you can't be sure. All you know is they represent what you will never become. Hopeless. His despair has made him a pariah. You consider approaching him, but you make no motions to do so.

Staring at the computer monitor, you think about work. Upon your arrival, Churchill got you a job and a home. From there, it was up to you to make something out of them. Like your flat, your desk features a memento from Topside life—a black and blue dreidel your mother handed to you as a child. You spin it, watching it tumble off the desk. Always a source of childhood enjoyment, but memories fade. Treasures now inherit the nightmares.

A door opens. All typing stops, as if someone has cut the cord. You ease up, peeking over your partition wall. Breath catches in your throat.

Expression sullen, face bearded, you watch Agent Lincoln wander inside. A question stands ready on the tip of your tongue, but Hope presses his finger to his lips. Why would an Agent of Despair come here? Agents wandering Rock Bottom before the Lonely Hour is a strange sight. The Weeper chokes back more tears, and your heart squeezes tight. Only emergencies summon agents before the Lonely Hour.

Everybody's head pivots, then looks away, fearful of catching his attention. But the agent's focus is trained on someone in the far corner like a bird spotting prey. The Weeper's cries intensify, whimpering like a child facing the wrath of a teacher wielding a cane.

"Don't look," Hope says, raising a hand to block his vison.

But it's too late. You are looking, *staring*, and you are hopeless to stop it.

Lincoln reaches out. At full stretch his sleeve pulls back, revealing the patch of skin between his gloved hand and shirt. Scaly flesh spots across his wrist, screaming like wraiths out of their graves. Your head begins to pound. Lincoln's fingers curl around The Weeper's head, blighting his face and silencing the whimpers.

Jaws unhinge and Lincoln bears pointed teeth.

"*Get down!*"

Yanked to the floor, you clamp your hands against your ears to kill the screams of a dead life dying.

Shadows thrash against the walls of your mind, breaking and coming together like ink in water. You see Lincoln breathing in the nightmares. His face, once sullen, looks pleasurable, like he's in the throes of an orgasm. Paper flutters around the office as the storm rages on. The Weeper screams and screams, and Lincoln breathes and breathes.

Something shakes you, but you don't dare look. You are shaken again, hard enough to hit your head against the partition wall. Eyes open, you see Hope, his face alert and afraid.

"Are you all right?"

No, you are not. Your brain is a state of decay, not from your own nightmares, but those of The Weeper's.

Hope announces he is taking you home. You grab his arm, telling him no. Your flat is a haunted house you don't want to revisit, but he insists, and you are powerless to resist.

The door bangs open, and he puts you on the patchwork sofa. He hurries out of the bathroom with a syringe and a bandage.

"Pull up your sleeve."

You don't protest. He seems to know what he is doing, and unlike you, he knows what's happening — why The Weeper's bad thoughts haunt your head. He wraps a tourniquet around your elbow, exposes a vein, and plunges the needle home. Ominous black liquid seeps into the syringe.

"Wha-what is that?"

"Quiet." He then replaces the hypo with a clean one filled with pale blue liquid, taps the needle, and floods the vein. You feel different. It's as if he injected a supercharged sedative into your system. The lights flicker. You look at Hope, begin a question, and then stop.

The lights go out.

6.
TRUTH

You cringe deeper into the mattress, determined to sink into it. Someone steps into the light, throwing their shadow across the wall. It's Hope. Relief comes, but a cold sweat follows in its wake. Any trace of optimism you felt on your way to work earlier that day has disappeared like a dream upon waking.

Hope brings the footrest from the sofa and places a mug on the nightstand. You can't be certain if he kept watch as you slept, but if he did, then he doesn't show it. His clothes remain as crisp as a morning frost.

"How are you feeling?"

Vacant rooms. You have nothing to say. He inspects the bandage wrapped around your forearm. It throbs a little, but it's your head that screams the loudest.

You lick your lips, gathering energy to talk. "What did you do?"

"Drink first." He hands you the mug of golden liquid. It tastes like honey. You sip again, and he takes it away, returning it to the nightstand. "Not too much. Post-Howl Insanity is still my concern."

"Post-Howl what?"

He flaps his hand. "Forgive me. I'm moving too fast, aren't I? Do you remember what happened at work?"

A cadence of tapping keys replays its melody. Calm colors swirl around like windswept ribbons, and birdsong pervades the background silence. Then the melodies die, and a black suit appears. An Agent of Despair. Was it Lincoln? You remember his sleeve pulling up. His scaly skin. You had shut your eyes, hadn't you, but The Weeper kept on screaming.

You tell Hope all of this. His expression is grave.

"You weren't supposed to see that."

"What was it?" you ask.

"A Howling," Hope answers. "It's what agents do when someone is showing extreme signs of depression, anxiety, and unhappiness. Weepers. In short, it's what agents do when people have given up."

"So, they kill them? To put them out of their misery?"

You can see Hope doesn't want to answer you, but you insist with a gesture.

"Let me tell you the truth about Agents of Despair, all right?"

You adjust where you sit on your bed, hiding your impatience.

"They are supposed to evaluate you to see if you can return Topside. But they don't want to. Churchill tried everything to disprove my recovery, but facts are facts. The handbook insists he let me go. But agents are not human. You probably know that."

Lincoln's screaming skin returns to mind. A sip of honey dulls the memory.

"They keep up an image of help to hide their true ambition."

"What's that?"

"Food," Hope says, and that one word scares you more than Lincoln reaching for The Weeper's face. "They feed on misery. They observe Topside and take miserable people from above. People who exhibit unhappiness. People like us."

"But don't people know?"

He shakes his head. "Sadness doesn't make one question how things work."

Your mind is confused, but you let him carry on.

"Anyway, It's people like The Weeper that agents like the most. It's like slow-cooking a stew for hours, and when it's ready, it's delicious. Rich gravy and meat melts in the mouth. When agents know these people absolutely cannot go on—perfectly cooked food—they eat them. They *do not* put them out of their misery."

You shudder at the thought of where The Weeper is now. Is he somewhere deeper than Rock Bottom? You sip more honey.

"How can you know all of this?"

"I'm a ghost. And a prisoner."

"A prisoner?"

He sighs and stands by the window. Snow continues to fall. "Churchill tricked me when he signed my acceptance form."

You say nothing, keen to hear more.

"When I went to the Topside lift, I handed over the sheet to the agent on duty, but he didn't grimace at me in contempt that I slipped through the near-unescapable system. He smiled. It worried me, and I was right. Because when the lift was about to break through the clouds, the world flashed white, and I was gone. I guess it's how people Topside feel the moment they are about to die, a sudden disconnectedness, perhaps. I was suddenly flung out of my body and falling back to Rock Bottom. For a moment, I saw color above and then sadness below." He turns, his face now a cracked porcelain vase. "I landed back inside my flat, now vacated, of course, and I understood what happened. The agents would never let me go." Hope leans against the wall, and you can see tears glistening. You want to pat his shoulder, to return the favor, but you are weak. Your head is murder.

"A little while later, you came in." He gestures at the door. "I tried to get your attention, but you went on looking at your new flat. That's when I realized I was a ghost, doomed to wander Rock Bottom in a personal solitude. I imagine the agents are waiting for me to fall apart so they can eat me, even if I am a ghost. But I won't."

You ruminate his story, thinking about the details.

"If you're a ghost, how come I can see you now?"

His lips curl into a smile. "Because I accepted who I was. Just like I accepted my situation before and decided to turn my life around."

You shake your head, unable to comprehend his confidence.

"Hope, don't you understand? The agents sent you back. You can't escape. If I try, they'll do the same to me."

To your surprise, he smiles wider.

"No, they won't."

"How can you know? *We're trapped!*"

"Agents of Despair have one weakness."

"What weakness?"

The smile is so wide you worry it will crack his face in two.

"Despair."

7.
BELIEVE

"**A**gents are not exempt from a Howling," he says. "What?"

You listen to Hope like a child enraptured by a story. He tells it with such encyclopedic accuracy that you are certain he knows everything there is to know here. But his plan jars like a tricky equation.

"Rock Bottom is designed to foster depression, but agents have a way of ignoring it." He shuffles forward, closing the gap between him and your bed. "Have you ever seen one smile?"

You recall seeing Van Gogh outside the Lonely Tower, his mouth sneering a lunatic clown's grin. Had he Howled someone? Was that why he was smiling?

Tremors rumble up your spine. "It was horrible."

"Agents have to fight through the pain," Hope says, "but sometimes, even for them, it becomes too much. As far as I know, there is only one thing that makes them fall into pits of sadness deep enough to earn a Howling."

You sit up, keen to hear the end of the story.

"You don't mean…to show happiness?"

He nods, no doubt pleased you know.

"It's one of the reasons why Churchill was hell-bent on disproving me. He was becoming depressed, even more so. The fact that I was able to show happiness, here of all places, was too much. So, to return balance to the world, he tricked me."

"So… are you saying we have to wait six months? My next appointment?"

"We can start tomorrow," he answers. "Trust me, when you tell the receptionist you are happy, Churchill will want to see you."

"But…" You grip the duvet like a child holding it for safety. "I'm not happy."

"It doesn't matter. We have to make him *believe*."

You think about your last attempts for salvation, each ending with a stamp painted red, and listening to heartbreak rock with the rest of the losers at Unhappy Hour. Have any of those barflies been Howled yet?

"Drink the rest of your honey." Hope moves to the kitchen. "From now on, I want you to focus on things that make you happy, all right? Anything."

The honey goes down warm and sweet. Your stomach hitches, but it settles, wanting more.

"Nothing here makes me happy."

"Topside then," he calls. "What made you smile?"

You are already thinking of them. Your wife, Sarah, playing in your daughter's room, making baby sounds and crashing toys together. Your daughter, Ellen, laughs with delight. You imagine walking to the park with them, Ellen in your arms. Everything was perfect, and everyone was happy. Then the car swings into view, smashing through the colorful image and *wham!* It's gone.

"Hey." You are shaken alert. Hope's holding another mug of steaming honey. "Are you all right?"

You want to lie and blame the drink, but the reality of what awaits tomorrow dawns on you with the shivering anxiety that's apt to follow. Lying won't help, and you know it.

"They died." Tears burn, ready to break free. "We were on our way back from the park when the car came."

Hope places the mug on the nightstand and sits on the footrest, leaning forward.

"They were walking ahead," you say. "Ellen was jumping for butterflies flying out of a garden. We had to cross by the bus stop before the blind gap ahead. Then Freddie Needham came out of his house, said hello, and slipped on an empty milk bottle." You sit up straighter, determined to get through this tearlessly. "The fucking milkman forgot his rounds, *again*. Poor Freddie sprawled on the ground, face first. He got his hands up in time to block the fall, but they were cut badly. I went to him, and I'll never forget what he said. 'Fucking cow-fuckers. I didn't retire early to fall flat on my snout!' He always made me laugh. He was a tough old guy. I think he used to work in MI5 or something like it. He had the *look* for it, you know?"

Hope nods, encouraging you to continue.

"I think Sarah and Ellen were so enthused with the butterflies that they didn't know I was behind. Then I heard the squeal of tires. A sound like that was weird on our street. I looked up and saw the car swinging around the bend way too fast, and—"

It's useless. The memory flowers, and the rains fall. Tears puddle your duvet, hot and long overdue. You can't stop. You heave in breaths, shuddering when you exhale. Hope rubs your shoulder, staying quiet, and that's all right. Right now you don't need his voice. His company is enough. You allow yourself time to grieve until The Weeper and Lincoln replace the pain. But it's hard. The tears want to fall.

"You don't have to go on," Hope says.

You laugh a little, accepting the irony. Wasn't he the one who advised you to talk about it when he saw the photograph of your family? The TV remote is still broken on the floor, a reminder of your refusal to explore the past. It hurts now, but deep down, it feels like a chain is slinging off your heart, unleashing trapped thoughts.

"It's okay," you say. "I have to say it, don't I? To accept it." He nods, his face akin to a mourner at a funeral, listening to a eulogy. "I saw the impact. I left Freddie on ground and dived over his garden, shouting their names. Sarah was on her back, and there was blood pooling out of her mouth. I tried first-aid, pumping her heart, but I knew from the sight of her, she was gone. When I looked up for help, I realized I couldn't see Ellen. People came out of their houses, and I asked them, shouted her name, screaming, 'Where's Ellen?' and people looked around. Then a cry came from the man two doors from Freddie's. He had his hand to his mouth, and he looked as though he'd seen a corpse in the bush. But then I realized, he *had* seen a corpse in the bush."

You cry again, and Hope rubs your shoulder.

"I understand," he says. "Quiet, now."

Now the floodgates have opened, you try to talk, but your throat hurts, and the pain of the worst day of your life is so horrific you want to pinch your face to get rid of it.

"You've done a brave thing," he tells you. "Acceptance is hard. I understand that. But now, you can start to believe." He observes your reaction. "Do you now understand why you are here? Why you are here in Rock Bottom?"

You nod. It feels like your neck can't support your head, as if your revived memories are weighed down by your spent tears. "Because the day my family died, I didn't want to live anymore."

He pats your shoulder again. It's a soft touch, and you welcome it like a remedy for an awful pain. "Exactly. The agents felt your misery and took you in your sleep. It's how they do it. There are dark machines in the Lonely Tower, and they have ways of reaching Topside. Through nighttime dreams, most likely."

His knowledge surprises you again. He could tell you the meaning of life, and you would believe him. Looking at his kind eyes, you realize you would place your life in his hands without thought.

"How do you know all of this?"

"When you are a ghost, you can see plenty of things," he answers.

You reach for his hand and squeeze. "Thank you."

He nods and pats your hand.

"Happy thoughts, okay? Tomorrow, we leave."

8.
HAPPY THOUGHTS

Happy thoughts are hard to summon when the world around you forbids happiness with eternal snowfall and steam-powered grates. You know Hope is watching you, following your every move, but the pull of depression tugs your sleeve like a seductive mistress, asking for your company. Work alleviates the pressure, but every now and then, your eyes drift toward the spot where Lincoln ate The Weeper.

Your fingers slip off the keys, breaking the melody. A hand touches your shoulder.

"Happy thoughts," Hope says.

You nod and resume typing, following the printouts.

Sarah occupies your thoughts. Her memory untouched by misery. Long blonde hair cascading down her shoulders like silk curtains. All the little things you loved about her return. The way she would place her umbrella in the crook of her arm to open doors on rainy days. Nudging hair behind her left ear when nervous. You can feel the smack of her lips when she kissed your cheek for no reason when you sat together watching TV.

Tides break, washing new memories ashore. Thoughts of Sarah flood into thoughts of Ellen. You remember her first word, and you and Sarah laughed out loud, thinking you had landed on your feet with this little one. Learning Mummy and Daddy came shortly afterwards.

The car swings around the corner, and then they are gone.

"You have to try," Hope says.

"I *am* trying."

You bow your head, fighting back newborn dread.

"Listen to me." Hope kneels beside you. You feel like a child failing his homework in front of his parents. "I've been here. I know this is hard. But—"

"Nobody told you—" You stop. Look around, check for signs of eavesdropping. Then, with your voice below a whisper. "Nobody told you to see Churchill today."

His face crumples, and you know you are right. Hope had time to recover, whereas you do not. Nothing stops you from waiting six months, but the need to rise again is stronger than the need to drink rejection. Part of you believes in yourself, but it's the other part you can't convince. The part that haunts your mind with family tragedy, and the pain of another rejection. There is no way you feel you can change in time. If you couldn't do it in the six months before an appointment, how do you expect to tonight?

"Let me tell you a secret," Hope says. "The moment you *believe* it, it will be easier. You just have to stand up straight, look him in the eye, and say, 'I am happy.' You have to keep insisting and insisting, and then it will crack. And you *will* believe. It's the only way out. Your happiness will make *him* miserable, but unlike when I did it, you will *keep* telling him well after he can disprove you. Hurt him so much he will *beg* you to go Topside." He pauses, staring at you. "Why are you crying?"

Images of Sarah and Ellen collide like asteroids. Topside gleams above, and the world below feels a million miles away. It's a fleeting feeling, and you know its lasting appeal is less than a minute, but the notion that you *can* walk the world again is so bright, you cry. It's so simple. A second life *is* possible, and it all starts with belief.

You try to answer, but Hope touches your shoulder. A parent finding hope in his son's eyes.

"Hold that thought," he tells you. "Hold on tight."

You try, but it slips away like rope burning through your hands. Readjusting your grip, you cradle the memory of Sarah lying in bed beside you, looking through the window at the starry sky. It divides into a constellation of thoughts. All of them happy, all of them perfect.

The end of your shift arrives with the relief akin to suffering the torture rack. Colleagues break away, heading for wherever their depression takes them. Home, bars, strip clubs, subway stations. Your destination watches over the city like a sentinel.

The Lonely Tower.

Agent Plath is still there. Tapping dead melodies. Mercifully, she looks up. No sign of recollection.

"Can I help you?"

Hope touches your shoulder. "You can do this."

You search for help. He nods his belief, and you believe him.

"I am happy."

9.
WORLD ABOVE, WORLD BELOW

Churchill swoops down like an eagle chasing wounded prey. Sharp eyes study yours with contempt, as if it is a crime to be happy. Then you remember what Hope told you. It *is* a crime. Agents can't eat rotten food.

He motions to the lift. None of you talk on the ride up, but you don't need to. You have done this before.

Four people sit in the waiting room. They lock eyes with Churchill as he strides past, scared of another rejection. He waves them away, telling them to rebook. You have become top priority.

The door shuts behind you. Churchill takes a seat behind his desk, gestures for you to sit. You obey and clasp your hands together, holding on to your firm resolve of confidence. Breaking Churchill is the only way.

The fax machine gobbles up papers, and he assembles them on his desk. His trusty stamp already painted red.

"Your next appointment is six months away."

No words present themselves. Panicking, Hopes speaks behind you.

"Tell the truth. Tell him how you feel."

You lick your lips. Churchill looks impatient, his eyes like a headmaster dealing with timewasters. His stamp rises, ready to reject.

"I'm tired of waiting," you say.

"Waiting for what?"

"To admit that I am happy."

It's like he's been pinched. You are somewhat sickened at yourself for enjoying his pain, but remembering what Agents of Despair do quickly blights your shame.

"I have been happy for a long time."

This time there is a low, guttural groan, and he looks at his desk. He palms the sheets, flattening them like material to sew. He looks at you. Energies shift. "I rejected you last time." A smile creeps along Churchill's thin lips.

"Happy thoughts," Hope says. "Keep at him."

"But…" you lick your lips again. Churchill does the same. "I have everything you want me to have. A job, a home, a life. Now I am happy. I want to go Topside."

He adjusts where he sits. For a moment, you swear you can hear the screams beneath his sleeves, but you look away.

"I have your mood reports," he jabs his finger on the sheets. "There is no change."

"At work, no. At home, yes."

"We don't make reports for home life."

"And I wonder why." Your words get the desired effect. Anxiety flares the whites of his eyes. "You design workplaces to foster misery, but at home, we have climate control." The peeling page of wallpaper flaps inside your head. "*Some* control," you add. "But we have the best chance of recovery there. *That's* why you don't report on home life. Because you would have to accept far more people than you already do. And you won't be able to Howl anymore."

Churchill's expression is one akin to someone shot in the leg.

"How — how do you know?"

"Twist the knife," Hope says like a maddened spectator at a blood-sport event.

"I saw you do it. Lincoln reached out, like this." You reach for Churchill's throat. He stumbles out of his chair, smacking the wall.

You launch off your chair, driven by a desire to leave. "*You eat us!*"

His hand goes for his heart, digging into his skin. "What do you want?"

"I want to go home. Topside!"

"I cannot allow that."

"You *will*. I know agents can Howl another agent if they have to."

"And they must make a big meal," Hope adds. "Like steak and eggs."

You glance at Hope.

Churchill emits a childlike scream, like he's been yanked out of bed by the monsters his parents denied were real. "*You?*"

"That's right," Hope says.

The horror show on Churchill's face is unlike anything you have seen before. His hands cover his eyes, crying low, mournful sobs. It's the sound of a ghost in a haunted house. He can't be far from The Weeper's state of despair, but it's Hope who twists the knife further, hell-bent on scaring him beyond compare.

"We are happy." He stands over the agent, talking like a schoolyard bully. "You are not. You will accept his leave, or you will die, sent to wherever people go after the Howling."

Another wave of sorrow escapes his mouth.

"I said," Hope grabs Churchill's sleeve and yanks it up. Hope stops, words dead on his tongue. The sight of Churchill's skin is enough to drive you insane. This close, you watch tiny mouths crying on his shimmering flesh, waving in and out of each other like bodies floating in a lake. You realize it's not Churchill crying, but his skin. People. So many people waxing and waning in his flesh, mouths rolling over mouths, screaming a hurricane shriek. To you, it looks like a picture of Hell.

"*Take it!*" they cry. "*Take it, and leave us be!*"

You press your hand against your own mouth, fighting back the urge to vomit. How many people has he eaten?

"No tricks?" Hope says.

"*None! Please!*"

"We can go and never return?"

"*Yes! Leave us be!*"

"We are happy. You are not."

"*LEAVE US BE!*"

Hope slips the agent's sleeve down, silencing the mouths. After scanning it, he hands you the sheet and the stamp — now painted green.

"You should do this."

You take the letter, careful not to cut your fingers on the edges. You lay it on the desk, grab the stamp like a gavel, and slam it home.

ACCEPTED.
Signed,
Churchill.

Hope pats your shoulder.

"How do you feel?"

You struggle for an answer. Somewhere between happy and unbelief.

"I don't know."

"Let's go." Hope ushers you away. "Before they come."

You follow the signs to the lift. No words are spoken, but your hands shake with the excitement of it all. Part of you wonders if there is still a trick printed on the sheet, small print unnoticed, but you reconcile those thoughts with the knowledge Hope had already checked. But still, you worry. If this isn't a trick, then what does it mean?

You are *going home.* The chance to start over glows like a faraway light in the dark. And behind it, two voices call your name. Cheering you on.

Standing by the lift doors, you recognize the Agent of Despair's crooked nose as Fry. You cradle happy thoughts, chin up and smiling.

"He's the one who let me go," Hope says.

Fry inspects the sheet, and for a horrifying moment, you believe he will send you screaming back to Rock Bottom, like he did to Hope. He doesn't. He steps aside, and the doors hiss open.

"Good luck," he says, without malice or laughter.

You step inside. The doors close.

The lift jolts upward, and dark clouds blur past, thinning as you ascend.

"You did it," Hope says with a smile.

Your eyes flood with tears. "I can't — I can't thank you enough. Is it really over?"

"Yes. It's over." He takes your hand. "It was a joint effort. But one you deserve. You take care now."

Worlds collide, blighting the void in particles. "What? No. You get to come as well. We're both accepted."

"*You* were accepted," he answers. "Not me."

Heavy rain washes away your newborn relief.

"This isn't fair," you say. "You got accepted, too!"

"I'm tired. There's nothing for me out there. I wanted to send you up. You deserve it."

"But you're free to go!"

"I *am* free," he says. "Free from Rock Bottom, and now, with the sky as blue as that," he nods at the window, "I can go."

You turn and see the sky *is* blue. The lift has broken through the clouds, and colors replace the gray world below. An ocean gleams sunlight, and a faint shape rises and falls along the horizon. Home waits.

You look back at him. "You mean, once you reach Topside, you're free to die?"

He nods again, smiling this time. "I can see my son. For that, *I* can't thank you enough." He pats your hand, and you mumble another futile plea for his company. He shakes his head.

"Have a good life. And always remember why you chose recovery."

The touch of his hand vanishes like vapor. His clothes shimmer and crumple onto the floor, followed by his trilby resting on the heap like a marker on his grave. Then, a whisper. A final goodbye.

Waves of despair sting your eyes, but you fight them back. Hope wouldn't want your tears, not after your ascension. Without him, you wouldn't be here. No. You are free, and the world wants you back.

The lift jolts to a stop, and the doors open, welcoming sunlight. A gust of ocean wind blows through. It feels beautiful. A lighthouse stands tall, and there is a rowing boat moored beside it.

For the first time since the world ended, you smile.

You are happy.

About the Author

Nick Barton is a speculative fiction writer living in a quiet corner of Somerset, England. His horror stories have been published in anthologies such as *Riding the Dark Frontier II* by Thirteen O'clock Press and *Enter the Apocalypse* by TANSTAAFL Press. When not writing, he is often found wandering Skyrim, dancing to The Beatles, or watching *The Lord of the Rings* — again. He also enjoys peanut butter sandwiches and Iron Maiden guitar solos.

Sunday the 15th

Luke Bandy

I do not understand why I can't get some peace and quiet.

There I was, laying in my bed on a Sunday night, just trying to get some rest. It had been a long weekend for me. I chopped wood, killed a few dozen animals, and my Bowie knife needed sharpening. It was an original Bowie knife with a twenty-inch blade. My father bought it at a pawn shop, and I killed him with it several years later.

I was trying to sleep when the noises woke me up. Giggling and laughing. Someone was having fun at my camp, and no one has a good time at my camp while I am around.

My camp has been abandoned since I murdered a bunch of counselors in '82. I can't exactly remember the reason why I did it, though. My memory gets fuzzier each time I come back.

I think it was the time the kids dug up my mother's grave. So, I followed them back to their cabins and murdered them one by one in the most inventive ways I could come up with. I'm a creative person, and I like to apply that in my work.

Anyway, this one girl I was chasing in '82 set up a trap, and I fell on a spinning buzz-saw. Don't worry though. I got better.

I woke up later and found that the camp had been abandoned. That's also when I discovered I was immortal. Or at least so far as I can tell I am. I think it is the universe's way of saying "I'm sorry I gave you shitty parents."

My father was a devil worshiper, and my mother smothered me growing up. She meant well, though. She was just scared for me because of my condition.

I was born physically disfigured and without the ability to speak. Later, we discovered I didn't feel pain, too. So, my mother never allowed me to go out because she thought people would make fun me, and my father was too busy with his devil stuff to pay attention.

Between the two of them, I never really had an honest chance at a real life, but we can't choose our family.

So, I did the most reasonable thing. One day I took my father's Bowie knife and...yadda yadda yadda yadda...now I live in an abandoned camp and kill camp counselors.

I hate camp counselors. They are the worst. They walk around thinking they are so great, but they are not. Just because they are cute, young, and had decent upbringings doesn't mean they can smoke pot and have sex all day long. Especially at my camp when I am trying to rest.

The laughing got louder, and I had to get up at this point. I have lost count of how many times this happens. The problem is that my camp has become an urban legend, and there is an actual functioning camp across the lake. It is called Camp Woodchuck or something lame like that. My camp was called Belltower Adventure Camp because there was a chapel with a bell tower, but the tower burned down when some girl I was trying to murder lit it on fire with me locked inside. I think that happened in '86.

Afterward, I painted over the "B" with blood and made it an "H." Now it says Helltower Adventure Camp. I thought that would help encourage the counselors from Woodchuck to stay on their side of the lake. Unfortunately, I ended up with more of them coming over. I killed two batches of counselors that year.

So, I knew it was time to get to work. I have an old maintenance uniform for these occasions. It is something that is easy to get the blood out of. I got dressed, put on my work boots, and grabbed my helmet. It was a football helmet I acquired from one of my victims. Before then, I wore a hockey mask, but there is nothing worse than getting hit in the back of the head with no protection. Even though I don't feel pain, it is still very disorienting.

I did add a dark visor to the front, though. It makes it a pain to see, but I like to keep my identity secret for privacy reasons. It is the same reason I never joined Facebook.

I checked myself in the mirror and made sure I looked menacing. I have a hulking frame and stand at almost seven feet tall. Adding the helmet and knife, I was absolutely terrifying.

I made my way out of the cabin and moved toward the sounds of the laughter. I had to go slowly because it was night, and my helmet almost blinded me. I didn't want to trip and fall. That would just be embarrassing.

I made my way to the dock first. Once camp counselors arrived, I had to make sure they couldn't leave. Their rowboat was quietly bobbing in the lake as they partied a long way down the lake shore. I grabbed a nearby tree stump and yanked it out of the ground, then tossed it into their boat. There was the sound of wood snapping as the large stump made a gaping hole in the bottom. The boat sank, and that was the end of any hope of them escaping.

I made my way back into the woods. It helped that this batch of counselors had started a fire. I could make it out in the distance and advanced toward the light.

I got closer to hear what they were saying, and I had to roll my eyes. Camp counselors were so stupid, and I hated the things they talked about.

"Truth or dare?" one asked as I stood at a safe distance.

There were five of them. One girl was a redhead with way too much hairspray. Her hair was huge. I mean, I'm a fan of the '80s. Those were some of my best years, but it is 2018. She danced around their campfire and flirted with all the guys.

The guys could have been cookie cutter versions of characters from a teen rom-com. You had your super good-looking athlete, the smart guy with glasses, and the funny, token black guy.

Then there was a cute girl that was much more conservative than the redhead. She was blonde and modestly sat on a log. She smiled uncomfortably at the redhead's dancing. She would be a problem for me. For some reason, conservative innocent girls have cunning survival instincts and have murdered me multiple times.

So, this was a typical roll call of Woodchuck counselors. There was The Flirt, The Jock, The Nerd, The Black Guy, and The Virgin. I'm not actually sure if she is a virgin, but typically they are.

"So, truth or dare?" The Flirt asked as she danced.

"Dare," The Black Guy said and took a sip of his beer.

"I dare you to say Mason Luger's name three times." The Flirt giggled and danced some more.

First, that is not my name. I'm not sure where these kids get their intel, but that is not even close to my real name. It's like these kids don't know how to use Google. They just hear or read something and never fact check it.

I shouldn't have complained, though. That was good for me. As a mass murder, I didn't want to have a big internet footprint. Also, identity theft is a serious problem these days.

Second, even if that was my name, I don't appear when you say my name three times.

"That's not the legend," The Nerd injected.

Thank god, I thought to myself. Someone has some sense. Nerds were always good for clearing up things.

"You have to say his name five times while closing your eyes and leaning face-first into a tree." The Nerd explained.

I brought my hand to my face, and there was a clunk as my heavy glove hit my helmet. I shook my head in disappointment.

"What was that noise?" The Virgin said.

"Don't worry," The Jock told her. "I'll protect you."

Have I mentioned how stupid camp counselors are? I'm not sure if it is because of America's crumbling education system or if it is from all the pot they smoke, but they are morons. Any sane person that heard a noise in a place that an alleged serial killer lived would pack their things and leave like their lives depended on it. Not camp counselors, though. Not only do they think that I am a legend despite the number of counselors that have disappeared here, but they stick around when clues pop up that I may be real.

"I'm not sure if I like it here," The Virgin said.

"It's okay. Why don't we go for a walk?" The Jock told her.

"Yeah, sure." she said.

The two of them stood up and made their way toward the lakeshore. Meanwhile, The Flirt stopped dancing.

"Are you just going to leave me here with these two?" She seemed jealous. I think she had a crush on The Jock. I have listened in on a lot of teenage drama and can just read the tension. It's a trivial skill, but one you develop in this line of work.

"The fire is about to go out," The Nerd said.

"Yeah, the two of us should go get firewood," The Black Guy added.

"So, all of you guys are just going to leave me here alone?" she whined.

"You'll be fine," The Black Guy told her. "It isn't like Mason is going to come out of the woods with a chainsaw."

Chainsaw? I thought. That is such an unwieldy weapon. Plus, it's gas powered and can stall. Not an efficient weapon of choice. I questioned where these kids get these stupid ideas.

The two guys went off into the woods, and The Flirt was left sulking by herself. Another fact about camp counselors, they always split up. I'm not sure if it is something in the water they drink or the food they make at Woodchuck, but it does make life easier for me.

Once I knew The Nerd and The Black Guy were far off in the woods somewhere, I slowly made my way closer to the campfire. The Flirt slumped onto a log and poked at the ground with a stick. I could hear her complaining about her friends as I hovered over her.

I hovered and hovered, but she didn't notice me. It was killing my vibe. So, I took a few more steps toward her. Still, nothing and I was two feet away from her. I couldn't understand how she didn't see me. It wasn't like I was trying to be inconspicuous.

So, I cleared my throat, and that got her to turn around. She saw me and screamed. Ah, I love that sound. There is nothing more musical than a terrified camp counselor screaming in fear. She walked backward as I approached. I moved slowly because I didn't want to trip on the log she had been sitting on.

The next thing I knew, she stumbled in the fire, and her hair burst into flames. Her head lit up like it was soaked in gasoline. Then I realized it must have been all that hairspray she used. She yelled in pain, and instead of stopping, dropping, and rolling, she ran around while her head was on fire. That made it even worse, and soon her whole body lit up like a torch.

It was the craziest thing I have ever seen. Eventually, The Flirt ran head first into a tree and knocked herself out. She managed to kill herself without my help. All I had to do was clear my throat.

I was still taking credit for it, though. These counselors need to know to stay clear of Helltower Adventure Camp. So, I cut her head off, stuck it on a stick, and jammed it into the center of the fire for her friends to find.

Then I sauntered back into the woods and waited at a safe distance. Another fact about camp counselors is that they have dreadful hearing. That Flirt could have screamed all night long, and her friends would be somewhere going, *"Did you hear something?"* and *"It was just the wind."* I am not joking either. I have heard them say those things.

It felt like I was waiting forever. Finally, The Nerd and The Black Guy came back. They went through the typical motions of "Oh God! What are we going to do?"

Then The Jock and The Virgin came back and said, "We thought we heard a noise."

Sure you did. That's why you rushed back so quickly, I sarcastically thought.

"We need to get out of here," The Nerd said.

Please do, I thought. *By all means. Leave me alone. Stop partying at my camp*. But I knew I couldn't let them leave at this point. They had to be taught a lesson.

"We can't leave. The boat is gone," The Jock said.

Thanks to some careful preparation on my part.

"So, we're trapped here?" The Virgin panicked.

"I can't believe the legends are true. Mason Luger is real," The Nerd said.

"Oh man, we are stuck, and a chainsaw-wielding maniac is after us," The Black Guy said.

Still not my name. Still not the weapon I use.

"Don't worry," The Jock reassured. "I've got a plan. We'll all split up and try to find a way out of here."

"I agree. Splitting up is the best plan," approved The Nerd.

The four camp counselors all nodded in agreement and walked off in separate directions.

Counselors make it way too easy sometimes. I didn't even move from where I was standing. The Black Guy walked straight toward me. I am not sure how he didn't see me. It's not like I was wearing camouflage. I kind of stood out, even though it was dark.

The Black Guy just bumped into me. Then he started to feel around my chest like I could be a tree or something.

"You are no tree," were his last words.

I typically like to get more creative with my kills, but I kept this one standard. I was tired and wanted to call it an early night. I slashed his throat, and he made a desperate gurgling sound as blood poured out of his neck. I brooded over him and waited for him to bleed out.

That'll teach him for drinking beer and having fun.

Then I heard a scream from a distance. That was good news. I regularly set up traps for these occasions. Sometimes it can help speed up the process, so I'm not killing people for five days straight. It is so much simpler if I can get it done all in one night.

The scream came from the direction of my bear trap pit. It is simply a hole with a bunch of bear traps inside of it. Sure enough, The Nerd was at the bottom. He was mangled from all the traps snapping shut on him. Bones protruded from his skin, and his head had landed directly into one.

I had the trap connected to a pulley system. That way I could easily get the body out and let it hang there like a marionette. So, I pulled up The Nerd's body and hung it from a tree by the bear traps. He looked like a morbid piñata, and I hoped his friends got a chance to see my handiwork before I killed them, too.

That meant there were only two left, but then I hit a snag. It took a while longer to find the next counselor. I checked every abandoned building on the property. I must have kept on missing them. I could imagine them leaving an empty cabin right before I got there.

I should have stayed in one place and waited for them to find me. That would have been the better decision, but it was too late at that point.

It frustrated me, because things had been going speedily so far. I was hoping to be in bed by midnight, but not at the rate I was going.

That's when I got lucky. There was the sound of some breaking glass. I was several yards away from the greenhouse and remembered that I had locked it. Someone was breaking in. I contained my excitement as I made my way toward the noise. There was one problem, though. The greenhouse was in a clearing, and I stood out, lumbering through the grass.

It was The Jock that was inside, and he must have seen me through the glass walls and had prepared for a fight. As I opened the door, he charged at me with a rake. The rusty tool plunged deep into my shoulder. I punched him in the chest, and he flew back several feet. I knocked the wind out of him and could hear him gasping for air.

Despite not feeling pain, getting stabbed with a gardening tool is not my idea of a good time. The rake was a nuisance to get out, too. Finding good leverage was impossible. I was stabbed in my right shoulder, and I'm right handed. Trying to pull the thing out with my non-dominant hand was proving fruitless, so I just snapped the handle off and figured I'll deal with it later.

That did make my right arm kind of useless until I could get the rest of the rake out, though.

It didn't help matters when I discovered The Jock just wouldn't die. When I went to finish him off, he was gone. I looked around but couldn't find him. I then understood how frustrated people got when I would disappear after being knocked down. Counselors just give me too much time to recover.

Then I realized I had made the same mistake. I internally swore for being so stupid.

Then there was a ceramic crash against the back of my helmet. The Jock had snuck up behind me and hit me with a pot. Of course, I was completely unharmed and stabbed him in his gut. He seemed surprised that the pot didn't work, but helmet beats pot every time.

The Jock stumbled back and clutched his wound. I slowly approached him, expecting him to have lost his fight, but he grabbed some gardening shears and lunged at me. Those stupid shears went six inches deep into my left thigh. The kid was starting to piss me off. So, I yanked out the shears and stabbed him in his left thigh.

Tit for tat, I thought.

The Jock's eyes lit up in pain, but he didn't go down. I had to admit, this kid was tough. Then he grabbed me by the rake stuck in my shoulder to steady himself. He had a good grip, and I got an idea. I grabbed his arm and used it to try to get the rake out. His wrist broke under my grip, but he thankfully managed to keep hold of the rake, and it came out of my shoulder.

The Jock screamed in pain as I rotated my right arm. There were some kinks, but I could use it again. With his good arm, The Jock smashed another pot on my head. I can't talk, but I shrugged my shoulders and used my hands to try and mime, *Seriously? That didn't work before. I'm wearing a football helmet. Why would it work this time?* I had to give him credit for his persistence, though.

Since I broke his left wrist, I broke his right one too. I get OCD with stuff like that. I just like things to be balanced. He screamed some more and fell to his knees.

I pulled back my knife and was about to finish off The Jock when the greenhouse filled with a bright light. My first thought was, *Wow. I can see a lot better now.* Then I realized they were headlights and a truck barreling through the greenhouse hit me at 40 mph. I could feel some of my ribs crack as the grill hit my chest and the tires ran over my body. Since I don't feel pain, it is kind of hard to tell if anything has been severely broken or if I have internal injuries.

I lay underneath the truck as someone got out.

"Come on. Let's get out of here," I heard The Virgin say. I looked over and could see her sneakers as she helped The Jock into the truck. I reached out from under the truck and snatched her ankle. She screamed, and the next thing I know, the gardening shears were stuck straight through my hand. She must have snatched them out of The Jock's leg as a knee jerk reaction.

I pulled my hand back and tore the shears out when the truck moved and ran over me some more. Lucky, I had gotten that rake out of my shoulder. Without my arm, I would not have managed to grab hold of the undercarriage as the truck rode off. I was dragged behind the truck for a while, but this wasn't my first rodeo. I knew not to panic and stay calm. It took some work, but I hoisted myself into the bed of the truck.

There was a loud metallic clang as I landed.

"What was that?" I heard The Virgin say from the cab of the truck.

"I think it was an owl," The Jock drowsily responded. He didn't sound right. Probably from all the blood loss. He deserved it, though. That'll teach him to try and have sex with a virgin at my camp.

I fleetingly wondered where the truck came from. Then I remembered it being stashed in the camp's garage. I could never find the keys for it, though. These are the moments I wish I could talk so I could ask where she found them. I'm such a curious person. I like to know the small details, but I knew it would probably remain a mystery to me.

I punched through the back window of the truck's cab. There was lots of screaming as I reached in and yanked hard on the steering wheel. The vehicle veered off and smashed into a tree. I was jolted out of the truck when we hit. I fell and landed on my head. Again, not feeling pain has its advantages, but I was still stunned. Everything went hazy, and I rolled onto my back and looked up at the stars. I didn't realize it before, but it was a beautiful night. I took a second to enjoy the moment. I didn't move and just lay on the ground and stared up through the trees into the evening sky.

I started to contemplate why I was doing this. Maybe it was better to just leave the counselors alone? The world is so big, and I had stayed at the camp for so long that I wondered if I had lost perspective. I had always wanted to see New York and imagined what Manhattan would be like.

Then those damned camp counselors came over and ruined my introspective moment.

They leaned over me and blocked my view. These two were making me mad.

"Is he dead?" The Virgin asked.

"I don't know." The Jock said. Then he got closer to me. I think he was trying to see if I was breathing. Who knows, though? I can never understand how camp counselors think. When The Jock got close enough to me, I jammed by Bowie knife into the top of his skull.

That's for blocking my view, I thought. That's another time I wished I could talk so I could deliver some witty one-liners.

The Virgin took off screaming as I pushed The Jock off me. I stood up, but my head was jumbled. Getting run over by, and then thrown off, a truck had taken its toll.

I searched around to see which direction The Virgin went. I saw the truck was bent around a tree. The headlights had gone out. That was inconvenient, because I could have used the light. I went over to the truck, and I managed to get the headlights back on.

The woods lit up, revealing the shadows of the trees. There was no sign of the girl or what direction she ran.

That's when I noticed visor in the truck was down. I could see the impression of the keys on the visor's padding.

Why did I never think to look under the visor? I thought to myself as The Virgin snuck up behind and stabbed me in the back with something. It surprised the devil out of me, and my first reaction was to awkwardly try to get it out of my back. I barely managed to grab it and yank it out. It was the wood axe from the back of the truck.

I threw the axe on the ground, frustrated with how careless I was being.

The girl had disappeared again. I looked around to see if I could find where she had dashed off to. The headlights didn't help. She was far gone now, and she wasn't screaming anymore, so I couldn't track her that way.

The truck had crashed close to the bridge that connected my camp and Woodchuck. It was closed off, and you couldn't cross it safely. In fact, I think the truck would have plunged into the water if it rode over the bridge. It was old and rotting, barely holding up its own weight.

The bridge was my best bet, though. The Virgin would most likely try to find a way back to camp, and the bridge was the only option. I ambled onto the dirt road the truck had skidded off and started toward the bridge. Out of the woods, I moved a little faster but still had to pay attention to where I was going. There were potholes along the road, and the last thing I needed was tripping on one.

I meandered my way and eventually made it to the bridge. It was quiet. I didn't see any signs of The Virgin. That was annoying. Now I wouldn't get to bed until well past midnight. This was not the way I wanted to be spending my Sunday night.

It was a long shot, but I thought maybe she crossed the bridge, and I could catch her on the other side. I'm not too crazy about leaving the camp. One day I'd love to travel, but I have this unwritten truce with the outside world. I wouldn't leave camp and go on a killing spree, but I get to kill anyone that invaded my territory. At least, I think we have a truce. It is the only reason I could come up with that explains why the cops never came around. It could also be because the cops were idiots.

The bridge creaked as I walked over it. Being a big man, I had to be careful. One of the boards could easily break if I stepped on it wrong.

I made it halfway across when it happened. The Virgin got me. Those virgins could be so crafty. Honestly, I was just impressed how often one of them kills me. This one was quite creative, too.

She was waiting underneath the bridge. The Virgin must have been some type of rock climber or gymnast to get under there. When I came by, she tossed a chain around my leg and closed it with a lock. I pulled on it, but I felt the wood of the bridge snapping under my weight. I was not the best swimmer, and drowning was a rough way to go, even for me.

Then I smelled it: gasoline. The bridge was soaked in gas. The Virgin must have gotten it from the garage. It only took me a moment to figure out what she was going to do. I looked up from the chain to see she had made it to the other side of the bridge.

She held a pack of matches, lit one, and dropped it onto the bridge. The wood caught on fire like a dry pine cone.

"Hope you enjoy the heat, Mason, because it'll be even hotter in hell!" she screamed through the fire light.

Mason is still not my name. *How did they even come up with that name?*

I watched The Virgin run to safety as I began to burn. The wood bridge made a single massive moan as it shuddered.

Great, I thought. *I am on fire and get to sink to the bottom of the lake, too.*

There was a massive groan as the bridge collapsed in on itself. Everything was chaos as my body bounced off burning debris in a free fall. In a split second, I smashed into the water and sank. Giant pieces of wood cascaded around me, pinning me to the lake floor.

I tried moving, but it was useless. The remains of the bridge had buried me. I laid there in the darkness, and my lungs filled with water. Drowning causes a person to panic, and that was what I did. It was terrifying, and it felt like an eternity to drown.

Eventually, it all ended. I faded away, but I knew I would be back. This was a stickier situation than usual, but I knew that someone would find me one day, and I would wake back up.

Then I would find a new batch of camp counselors and start the cycle all over again. Maybe one day I'd leave the camp, though. I still wanted to see New York. Maybe I wouldn't wake up for a few centuries? That would be weird. I wondered what the future would be like.

So, my body lay in the water, patiently dead, as I awaited my return.

About the Author

Luke Bandy is a world traveler, teacher, and storyteller. He is a graduate of the Long Ridge Writers Group and has earned his master's in secondary education. Recently, Luke returned from Prague where he taught English and creative writing. He now resides in Baltimore, MD. More of his work can be found published in the Adelaide Literature Journal and at www.lukebandy.com.

NIGHT DRIVE

Gwyneth Cooper

Mike swung himself into the car as people waved and called out goodbyes from the porch. The car was cold, and the engine turned over reluctantly, coughing to life and then roaring rough as gray smoke spread over the wet grass. There would be a frost in the morning, but right now it was just the bitter, bone-deep cold of midnight and the Southern Cross hanging unforgivingly in the sky. Flicking his lights on, Mike backed up, tires crunching on the gravel. He unwound his window and leaned out.

"Great party," he called one last time. Dave, standing on the porch with a cigarette, raised his hand in acknowledgement. Mike grinned and put the window back up. The heater was wheezing, but there was only a steady stream of tepid air on the front windscreen, no heat yet.

He glanced over into the passenger seat as he pulled down the driveway with a showy spin of his wheels, more to the middle than the left. Paula was curled there, arms crossed over her chest and shivering slightly.

"Dave didn't say goodbye to you," he said.

She shrugged.

"I was waiting for you," she replied.

Paula's lipstick was messy, and Mike imagined that half of it was smeared down his neck and over his collar. He didn't care. She looked almost ghostly in the dashboard lights, blue on her white skin and dark hair. She twisted awkwardly as she crossed the seatbelt over her chest and clicked it shut. Her breath plumed in front of her from the cold. They still had another twenty minutes to go to get home; Mike's feet were freezing in his sneakers and thin socks. He could only imagine how cold Paula's must be, elegantly arched and bare in her high heels. Mike loved how it made her stand, the curve it gave to her legs.

"Are you going to have frostbite?" he asked.

"If I say yes, will you have to massage my feet to encourage circulation?" She giggled, and he watched as she smoothed her hand down her thigh and over her bare knee. The soft sound of her roughened palm over satin made his mouth go dry, and he wrenched his attention back to the driveway as he turned out of it and onto the road. He couldn't wait to get home where it was warm and dry to strip Paula out of her dress and let all her party finery drop to the floor before pushing her into the shower. He loved her like this, satin dress and precarious heels with her mouth and eyes painted dark, but he loved seeing her bare and stripped down too.

"You just want me to suck on your toes," he retorted. "I know about how you get what you want."

Her giggle was infectious, and he found himself grinning at his hands on the wheel, at the white line painted down the road for him to follow. The truth was that he loved every part of her, would do whatever she wanted so long as he got to touch her. He glanced over again at the dry rasp of a lighter, watching her drag in the first filthy breath. Her cheeks hollowed, and her lips pouted. She cracked the window open and sent the smoke streaming toward it, but the remnants eddied around them both. He breathed in the acrid smoke hungrily, feeling the harsh taste of second-hand tar on his throat like a caress from her fingertips. Imagining that he could feel where it had touched her skin, her lungs, each cell it had moved over as she sucked it in and expelled it. It was like touching her, mediated by intangible smoke.

She turned the music up, tinny and crackling from the cheap speakers. It mixed with the smoke to surround them, bracketing them against the cold, clear, unfriendly air outside. Paula sang along, low-voiced and rough. He didn't care that her voice cracked and wavered; it matched the jolting of the car, the way he maneuvered it around corners. One hand clutching her cigarette, Paula used the other to slide over the satin of her dress again. He couldn't look, had to concentrate on the asphalt and the white line, but he knew what her thighs would look like, outlined in her red dress and curled on the seat. The words of the song were perfect for the night drive, as sharp as the wind that rattled the car and as slow and slurring as the sound of the wheels on the road. Guitars made layers of sound, the driving bass and drums steady underneath, as steady as Mike's heartbeat.

"I could've danced all night with you," said Paula. "You and me under the stars."

"You're so romantic," said Mike. He thought of the party they'd been to, the way she'd ground against him on the tiny makeshift dance floor to the wailing guitars of the shitty band. Her lipstick had been waxy on his mouth, her tongue and teeth rough on his neck, and her breath heavy with whiskey. "I could have taken you upstairs and fucked you in the bathroom."

"While someone was passed out in the bath?" she asked. "You'd like that, knowing that they could open their eyes and watch what you were doing to me."

Mike hummed and licked his lips, knowing that she'd be watching the gesture, maybe mirroring it. Tasting the synthetic cherry of her lipstick on his own mouth was like tasting her again, spit-slick and kissing messily.

"You're so dirty," she said, laughing. "What a filthy fucking boy. You'd love it."

"Don't even front," said Mike. "You'd love it too." She would, he knew, she'd arch her back and moan, not even trying to be quiet. She'd want everyone to know what Mike was doing to her. He kept his gaze on the road, his eyes away from her blue-ghosted face and smeared lips that looked black in the dimness. He knew what she'd look like; he needed to drive and get them home. Then he could tumble her onto the bed and kiss her, pallid cold taste of old lipstick on his tongue over the ashy residue of cigarettes.

He knew this road well. He loved the familiarity in the way it curved up and over the hill and down to where they'd turn right into the valley road. The party had been at the old McGregor place, hosted by young Dave, who lived in the sharemilker's cottage. Dave had gotten some shitty band to come out from town, all tight jeans and smirking smiles. They were town kids, studying music at the polytech and thinking they were something special.

Mike didn't care about that either; there was a keg, and Paula hadn't left his side. The songs they played were loud, riffs that had soundtracked a thousand parties, songs that everyone could sing along too. If he twisted back to look, he knew he'd still be able to see the lights of the house, high up on the ridge. There had been talk of a bonfire when they left, the city boys long gone. This place was home to Mike. He knew the dark loam of the soil from the way it tasted under his fingernails as well as from how it lay rich on the bright green grass as he shoveled it up to dig post holes. Underneath was stubborn clay, and he knew about that from kilometers of drainage ditches and long hours of throwing metal into them before laying in the half pipes and covering them over like mass graves. The soil was in his bones, worn right through his skin and muscle. He'd been born here. So had Paula. She understood the black soil too.

"You're getting melancholy," she said. She pushed the cigarette butt out the window so it flew off in the slipstream in a shower of red sparks.

"Just thinking of the hills and the road," he said.

"Remember when it was all gravel from the turn off to the sea?" she asked. "You fell off your bike at the school gates."

"I still have scars from the gravel," he said. "It wouldn't come out of my skin."

"Bullshit," she said. "I know all your scars. I gave you half of them." Mike shifted in his seat, and his back rubbed on the cracking vinyl, reminding him of the scratches she'd put down it, old ones mixed with the fresh.

She'd held his head still as they danced so that they could kiss, her fingernails digging red-pink crescents hard into his neck. As she shifted, they had scraped over old bite marks, and she'd laughed as he had moaned into her mouth. She'd always been a dirty kisser, ever since he was fourteen years old, and she'd pushed him against the wall outside the classroom of the tiny local school.

"Your scars are the deepest of all," he said. He glanced over, trying to read her face and failing. She had it turned away as she let the window down a little further and lit another cigarette. He let his gaze linger on the way her twisted torso exposed her breasts, pulling her dress tight over them.

"The road's empty tonight," she said. "I'd suggest you pull over and fuck me in the back seat, but that would just be a cue for the cops to turn up."

"Fuck," Mike said. He could totally see it, twisted up on the splintering vinyl with her ankles over his shoulders, cramped and sweaty, as satisfying and furtive as the first time they'd done it. "And you say I'm an exhibitionist. At least people in bathtubs are passed out."

"Oh, he wouldn't see any of me," said Paula. "Just your sweet little lily-white arse poking up like an invitation."

"Stop," said Mike. "The community constable drinks with my dad. I don't want to think about that." Paula laughed, and Mike risked another glance at her. She had moved and half her face was obscured. For a moment, she wasn't human, just a dark shape on the other seat, waiting for him to stop the car. Then she would take him and eat him up, absorbing him into her shadow. He shivered and concentrated on the white line and the sweet and certain curves of the road.

"Just kidding, baby," Paula said. Even her voice was unearthly for an instant, dry and rough as she exhaled, but then she moved, leaning forward and shifting her hand from her lap to his. The scrape of her palm cut straight to his nerves, even through his jeans. He glanced at her again, at her dark eyes and the bluish glow to her skin, but then her hand slid up, and he barely bit back a groan. "Keep your eyes on the road," she said. She blew out a stream of smoke that drifted round them both before swirling out the crack in the window.

"Fuck you," he said, ignoring the press of her fingers with an effort.

"You wish," she said. "You have to get us home first."

Mike swore under his breath, ignoring her laughter, and took the turn into the valley road too fast. She slid across her seat and against the door with a thud, her hand falling from his lap to rest back on her thigh.

"I love it when you're impatient for me," she said. Taking one last drag on her cigarette, she pitched it out the window. Rolling it up blocked the hiss of the wind, making the music sound louder in response. The car felt more intimate, like Mike could reach out and get right inside Paula if he tried.

The road was narrower now, but he'd spent his youth on it. He knew this, even without a line to follow. He liked it better this way, the way driving on it relied on his knowledge of this place and how deep that went. Paula was like that too. He couldn't remember a time she hadn't been next to him, as solid and changeable as the land around them. He set his car flying down the narrow strip of asphalt. He'd get them home soon, and they'd be able to shut themselves in his room. They'd have to be quiet, or at least try. He loved it when she muffled her moans in his shoulder or in his sheets. Later, he could press his face to the cotton and imagine she was moaning for him all over again. He could imagine that she surrounded him, every sloughed-off skin cell a caress.

He left the car parked haphazardly on the gravel to the side of the car shed. It wouldn't be blocking anything in the morning. Paula laughed as he pulled her from the car, towing her impatiently toward the house and warmth. A morepork called from the trees as they stumbled over the loose gravel. The noise made Mike shiver. He'd never liked the sound of the little owl, haunting and predatory. He tugged on Paula to move faster, even as he laughed over nothing into the skin of her neck.

A light burned above the door, and even though Mike knew his parents would be asleep my now, he still put his hand over her mouth to stifle the giggles as he fumbled his key into the lock and got them both inside.

It was darker here than it had been in the car. When Mike switched off the light, Paula slid into his space, plastered against his back with fingers twined in his belt loops. Mike's feet were still cold and wet, but the rest of his body was on fire. He stumbled as he turned and pushed her up against the wall by the door, kissing her through the taste of cigarettes and beer.

"Let's go to bed," said Paula, pulling away from Mike's mouth. Her head banged against the wall as Mike bit his way down her throat. Her skin was cold and white under his teeth.

"Yes," said Mike. His voice was muffled in her skin, and his hands felt like they were burning, anchored on her hips.

"You have to let me go," she said. His fingers tightened harder, maybe leaving bruises on the yielding marble of her skin. His mouth watered to get her clothes off and see, adding dark mouth marks over purple-black fingerprints.

"Not going to happen," he said. She laughed and pushed him away enough to start toward the stairs. He watched her go, letting her walk far enough ahead that he could watch the sway of her hips in her red dress, the vulnerable curves of her ankles above her high heels. She turned as she got in the door of his room, hands moving to the back zip on her dress as he kicked the door shut behind them.

Mike woke up alone in dirty sheets, face down and drooling into the creased cotton. His face felt sticky and squashed oddly, and he could smell the stale alcohol creeping from each pore. Shivering, he pulled the blankets tighter round his chin and turned over. The morning sun, even winter pale, still hurt his eyes. Somewhere in the house, a stereo was playing classic rock, and Mike's mouth watered for an instant coffee like his mum made for him, sweet and hot, made with milk heated in the microwave on top of the boiling water. She might make him a steak and egg sandwich for breakfast, maybe with mushrooms, definitely with too much butter. It would be greasy and sit in his belly perfectly.

Stumbling downstairs, scratching his stomach absently under his thick woolen jersey, Mike found both his parents in the kitchen. He ambled in, happy that he'd stopped in the bathroom for a quick shower and some painkillers for his headache. The tiny red pills in the little prescription bottle next to the painkillers mocked him, tempted him. He ignored them. He didn't need them, no matter what the doctors said. They didn't know shit about him and his mind; there was nothing wrong with him. He was young and invulnerable, not crazy. Not crazy at all.

The morning sun was stronger in the kitchen; Mike sat with his back to the window. His father had the newspaper open in front of him and hay in the creases of his pants, mud caked red round the hems.

"Thought you were going to sleep the whole day away," Neil said, not looking up from the paper. "It's good you're up. A branch came down on the gate in the top paddock. You'll need to go out this afternoon and fix it."

"Would you like a coffee first?" asked Raewyn. "I was just about to make one for your father."

"Yeah, sure," said Mike. He slid into his seat. "Did you see Paula this morning?" he asked. The newspaper rustled loudly as his father turned a page, but he didn't say anything. His mouth was turned down in a thin line. Looking at his mother, Mike watched her get a cup down from the hooks that hung under the cupboards and spoon in the coffee and sugar. She kept her back to him as she switched on the jug and got the milk from the fridge. Her spine was very straight, and it looked like her hands were shaking a little. The glass measuring jug went into the microwave, and she stood there and watched it as it spun round. The sound of the boiling water filled the room. A fly buzzed uselessly on the table by Mike's hand, a fat bluebottle that gleamed sullenly in the light. It climbed up over his finger, and he flicked it off. Circling round, it came back to rest near his hand again.

"Well?" he said. His mother poured boiling water onto the coffee and sugar mix. Retrieving the milk from the microwave, she wrapped a tea towel round the hot glass handle and poured it in carefully. She set the mug on the table by his hand. The fly flew out from under it just before it touched.

"No, I haven't seen her," she said, voice uneven. His father's newspaper rustled disapprovingly.

"Huh, I wonder when she left then," Mike said. "She better not have taken my car."

"Breakfast?" asked his mother. "I can make you a little something."

"Yeah, like bacon and eggs," he said. "Hash browns. It's surprising that Paula left. She likes your breakfasts as much as I do." He smiled at his mother, expression turning to a frown as she turned away to fuss with the tea towel, threading it in and out of the rail that it usually hung from, before smoothing it down and moving to the fridge. Neil put his tea cup down with a thump and lowered his newspaper.

"It's been years," he snapped. "Years since she—"

"Stop," said Raewyn. "Stop, Neil. We're not supposed to tell him."

"These doctors don't know shit," he said. "Look at him, Raewyn. We're not doing him any favors wrapping him up in cotton wool. He's old enough now; should be over that."

"Don't say it," said Raewyn. "You know they said it was the accident last week that triggered this."

Mike looked between them uncomprehendingly. His father looked angry, but his face was tired, and there were fresh lines carved there, lines of weariness and grief. His mother's back was still tense, the tremor in her hands more pronounced. When Mike closed his eyes for a moment, the only sound he could hear was the buzzing of the fly. Even his parents' breathing was gone.

"What's the problem?" Mike asked. "I feel fine." Neil pushed back from the table, scraping the legs on the floor. The fly circled down to roost on Mike's cup.

"I don't believe we're doing anyone any favors," Neil said. "We're just letting him get worse. Four years, Raewyn. Four years, and we're back to this when he tips off the gravel in the race and into the ditch. A tiny little accident and we're right back where we fucking started." Raewyn twisted her hands together in front of her, and when she turned, Mike saw her eyes were shiny. Neil pushed his chair in with a grating noise and slammed the door behind him on his way out. Mike looked between the blank door and his mother, blinking as she turned back to the fridge and pulled out the bacon, pink and squashy in its plastic packet.

"Seriously, what's the problem?" Mike asked.

"Nothing," said his mother. "Nothing, it's fine."

Mike was sure he'd feel more human after breakfast and a second coffee. He watched his mother move in jerky, uncertain increments, taking in her fragile movements as she started the bacon sizzling on the stove. The bluebottle buzzed sluggishly next to his coffee, and he slapped at it lazily. It squashed under his palm with a squelch and a smear of iridescence and guts. With a disgusted grunt, he got up to wash his hands and wipe the table.

Paula had her face tipped up to the mid-afternoon sun as she leaned on his car, feet crossed at the ankle and hands in the pockets of her faded jeans. She didn't move as Mike boxed her in, hands on her hips just above the waistband of her jeans.

"You were gone when I woke up," he said.

"I couldn't sleep," she replied. "I had to go home and change anyway."

"I missed you," Mike said.

"You were drooling into your pillow when I got up," she said. "I didn't miss you." Growling, Mike bit her neck as she laughed.

"I have to go fix a gate," he said. "Want to come?"

"Spending time alone with you?" she asked. He slid his hands up under her jersey and T-shirt, scraping rough over the skin of her waist. "I think I could handle a little of that," she said. This time, he laughed into her neck.

She slid into the bench seat of the ute with a smile. Her lips were perfectly red again, dark and shiny against her white skin. Mike wanted to taste her lipstick, messed up and smeared like a bruise as her lips grew swollen and tender from his kiss. He pulled out of the yard and into the main race with a flurry of cold dust.

He'd driven the race a thousand times, more, from when he was young and perched on his father's motorbike in front of him, to when he learned to drive the old diesel when he was ten. In winter, mud overlaid the gravel in wet weather, and in summer, the dust rose to choke him. He'd spent long hours in the sun spreading the loose metal over the old ruts of the ground, longer hours on the bike behind the cows as he moved them or brought them in for milking. He knew all of this land, each loose bank of earth and each dirty scar of slips on hillsides.

As he dragged the wheel round to make the sharp turn that would take them up the ridge, his eye caught on the marks of tires down the bank and into the ditch. At the bottom, the edge of the ditch was ripped raw and there was new wire in the fence. Next to him, he couldn't even hear Paula's breathing. The truck shuddered to a stop as he felt suddenly sick.

Leaning out of the door, Mike let the nausea catch up with him. The vomit poured out of him, bitter and vile. He remembered waking up in hospital with the white sheets pulled tight over him and his body aching. He'd felt so small in the narrow bed, before the last of his teenage growth spurts. Just nineteen, driving to the beach in the wet in his father's ute, bright and cocky in the gray drizzle. He could remember the twist and slide of the truck as it slipped on a turn, wheels spinning uselessly on fresh wet metal on the road to the sea. Paula's lipstick smelled of cherries, but her blood was coppery flat and slippery as she slumped into his side as the truck came to a stop upside down in another ditch. The rushing of the water just under the roof had sounded louder than the hammering of his heart. It had muffled and drowned his begging and cries. He remembered the dead weight of her body and how she'd not responded to his voice, even as he ran his hands over her, waiting for the ambulance to come. Her blood had sunk into his clothes, over his skin. He could sometimes taste it in his mouth, even when they hadn't been kissing hard enough to split his lip.

Shaky and sick, he finished vomiting up everything left in his belly in a foul heap of beer and bacon onto the grass. He didn't straighten up, terrified of seeing Paula in the corner of the cab with her limbs twisted up and drenched in caking blood. The hand that came to rest between his shoulder blades was cold and heavy on his shivering skin. The smell of her cherry lip gloss floated sweet to his nostril, and he heaved fruitlessly, trying to rid himself of all the poison in his body, all the toxins in his mind.

"Feeling better, baby?" she asked. "I'm right here for you, just like I always am. I'll never leave you."

About the Author

Ko au te awa, ko te awa ko au

Gwyneth Cooper is a teacher and crafter from New Zealand. She lives by the sea and drives those long gravel roads that rise and fall like the swells.

LIVESTOCK AUCTION

Brooke Reynolds

Ten-year-old Riley watched as the New Mexico early morning sun beat down on the creature. Its eyes were wide, and froth formed at its mouth; its lungs pushed with every last exhausted effort. With each struggling kick, the tangled barbed wire fence cinched down tighter around its legs and neck, biting into its flesh. Dust kicked up in a cloud and stuck to its sweat-drenched hide. A semi-circle trench formed in the dirt from feet that repeatedly pawed the earth as they searched for purchase. Its voice bellowed out a choking gurgle. Riley knew the creature didn't have much time left, so she hurried to fetch her papa.

She ran across the field and back up toward their simple two-story farmhouse. Her feet and arms pumped as fast as they could, the skin of her heels rubbed against the inside of her black rubber boots. She raced into the kitchen, and the screen door slammed shut behind her. Mama was there fixing breakfast.

"Don't be dragging mud in all over my clean house. You leave them boots at the door."

Riley's lungs heaved. "Where's Papa?"

"Out in the parlor milkin' with your brother. Did you finish your mornin' chores?"

Riley flew back out of the house and around back to the milking parlor. She had to find her papa. Maybe there was still time to save the poor creature.

The hiss and sucking sound of the milking claw being applied to each udder greeted her when she entered the parlor. Her nostrils filled with the tangy, sugary smell of sweet feed mixed with cow manure. The humid air engulfed her, making it difficult to breathe.

Some country singer singing about old dusty roads blared over the speakers. Papa said the music calmed the cows.

The parlor was a herringbone style, the cows positioned perpendicular on either side of the central pit. Riley watched as her papa and brother worked back to back in the pit, dipping each teat and wiping it clean before attaching the silver-fingered claw with the vacuum seal. White milk filled the canister below before being sucked away. Riley ran up behind her papa and pulled on his shirt. She shouted over top the radio and pointed in the direction of the struggling animal. Papa motioned for his son to keep working and followed Riley out of the parlor.

They stopped briefly in Papa's office for him to grab a pair of gloves, wire cutters, and his .22 rifle before heading down the hill toward the screams. Riley galloped off, and her papa trudged behind her.

When they arrived, the animal was on its second wind, kicking and flailing with all its might. But each kick led to another tangle. Riley approached and watched as flies landed on its face, surrounding the eyes. The creature tried to blink them away.

Papa sat the rifle down. Papa always had a way with the animals. He could calm the wildest of steers and the most stubborn of swine. It was like he spoke their language. With this animal, he was no different. He laid his hands on the beast, and it stilled. Riley took a step forward.

"Riley, stay back."

Papa didn't have to ask her twice. She watched as he went to work, cutting the barbed wire from around its neck, loosening the tangles so it could breathe a little easier. He reached down to start on the legs and stopped. He threw the wire cutters onto the grass.

"Dammit all to hell."

Riley went to retrieve the wire cutters. She tried handing them back to her papa.

He shook his head. "No, they won't do. Damn leg's broke." He pointed to the leg. "See how the bottom is twisted up like that. The foot's cold too. Probably lost circulation awhile back. From the looks of how deep this trench is, this poor thing's been out here all night."

"I came and got you as soon as I found it."

"I just can't figure how it got down in this field in the first place. He's one of the new ones I bought last week. I thought they were all still locked up in the barn."

Riley kicked at the dirt at her feet. She may have forgotten to lock the gate last night. She wasn't supposed to be in that area of the barn. She wasn't old enough. But she was curious and wanted to see the new animals.

"Riley? Did you let him out?"

She remained silent. Her papa could catch a lie faster than anyone she knew.

"Riley?"

Tears started to well in her eyes. She looked up at Papa. "I was just curious. You never let me see the new stock."

"You're too young. Now run on up to the house. I need to put this creature out of its misery. I'll deal with you later."

"Can't you fix it? Mama could call Dr. Kidwell?"

"He can't do anything for it. Animal like this is of no use with a broken leg. It ain't worth the cost to fix it. Now run on up to Mama."

"I can watch."

"Maybe next time. Now get going. Don't make me tell you again." He walked over and picked up the rifle.

Riley turned and headed up the hill. She still wanted to watch but instead listened to her papa. When she was almost at the house, she heard the animal let out one more deep moan. Then the crack of the rifle made her jump, and all was silent.

Later at dinner, Riley sat at the table with her brother and parents. They dined on short-ribs with gravy and creamy red-skinned mashed potatoes. Riley stared down at the ribs. She didn't have much of an appetite.

Mama addressed her. "What's wrong sweetheart? Eat your dinner."

She swirled the gravy around in the center of her potatoes. Papa still hadn't dealt out her punishment yet. In fact, he hadn't spoken to her for the rest of the day. Granted, Riley did her best to avoid Papa when she knew he was mad at her. She dipped her fork deeper into the potatoes and licked the tiny morsel off.

Mama continued to spark conversation in an otherwise silent dinner. "Should we rent a movie for tonight?"

Papa responded. "Can't. I have to get a fire going to burn the remains of that carcass. And Riley needs to get to bed because we're leaving early tomorrow for the fair."

Riley dropped her fork and looked up at her papa. This was a complete turn of events from what she expected. She figured the sentencing would include months of extra chores. She never dreamed a trip to the fair with her papa would arise from her mistake. "Really?"

"That's right," said Papa.

"Can I get some cotton candy? The blue kind? Not any of that pink stuff. Alex says they all taste the same, but I don't think so."

Her brother Alex responded. "It's just dye. Sugar is sugar. It all tastes the same."

"He's a liar."

Her papa interrupted. "No one is getting any cotton candy. This is a work trip. We're going to the livestock auction. Riley decided she was old enough to let the new ones out of their pen last night, and we lost one of our most promising stock."

There was the punishment. She knew freedom wasn't that easy. But still, she had begged for a trip to the fair with her papa for as long as she remembered. Even if the trip didn't end in any sugary delights, she was still happy to go.

"Do you really think she's old enough?" Riley's mother asked her papa.

"Alex was about her age when I took him. It's time she learned about the family business and how work gets done 'round here."

Papa parked the Silverado in the open field at the back of the convention buildings for easier loading. Hitched behind them was a small horse trailer, stainless steel with rusty and worn spots, and several wire cages of varied sizes lined the interior. In the distance, the bandstand's music filled the space around the towering Ferris wheel. Riley considered asking to ride but refrained. This was a work trip.

They walked around to the front of the convention buildings. There were four of them all together, each one uniform in size and shape. Papa spotted her eyeing the great wheel from a distance. "Work first. If there's time at the end, you can choose one ride to go on."

"When does the auction start?"

"Not for another hour or so. Your mother wanted me to pick up a few supplies, so we'll start with the far building and work our way down."

Riley fell in with her papa's footsteps. The first building they approached had its doors propped open. Vegetables of all shapes, colors, and sizes spread across the individual tables inside. They stopped at one particular table that contained jars of assorted honey. Riley loved spreading the sweet sticky nectar over top hot biscuits straight out of the oven. A woman standing by offered free samples. Riley looked to her papa, and he nodded his approval. She tasted three samples before choosing the darker, buttery Avocado variety.

They continued up and down the rows. Papa paused at a table offering information on robotic milking. Papa said a robotic milker would save them hours of labor, but they didn't have the funds for it. Still, she watched him accept a brochure. They continued on down the line and out of the building into the hot sun.

Riley's eyes adjusted as they made their way into the next building. Building two included a hodgepodge of critters, everything from sheep and pigs to chicken and rabbits. They walked up to the chickens and stopped. Papa turned to address his daughter. "All right, kiddo. I'm going to teach you how to pick out the best animals. This is an important trait to learn. It takes practice, so don't worry if you don't get it right away. Your mother wanted a few egg layers, so we'll start with the chickens. Check them over and tell me what you see."

Riley walked back and forth, assessing each of the birds. Black, red, white, and a variety of browns filled the cages. The ones with fat chests sat in their cages, eyes closed and drifting off to sleep. A few were tall and skinny. They strutted back and forth, pacing the small enclosures, pecking at the wires. Some of the chickens appeared to be wearing hats, the tops of their heads crowned with feathers that jutted out in various directions. Some were huddled in the backs of their cages with chunks of feathers missing.

Riley pointed at one of half-naked chickens. "We don't want these."

"Good," her papa responded. "Why not?"

"They look sick, like something's wrong with them."

Papa nodded. "That's right. Now when you're looking for good egg layers, the fatter the better. These skinny ones are too hyper. They're bound to run off and get hit in the middle of the road. Better to have one that's a little slower, so we can catch them if they escape."

Papa approached two identical-looking chickens. Each was a blend of reds and browns that bled into one another, their heads framed with short waddles. Both sat in the center of their cages. He pointed at the birds. "These are what we're looking for, Golden Comets. Fat breasts and clear eyes. They're curious but not scared. Plus, they lay brown eggs instead of white, your mother's favorite."

Riley took note while her papa made arrangements to purchase the chickens. She reached her fingers into the cage of the first bird and stroked the smooth feathers. The chicken pecked at her finger, drawing a single drop of blood. "Ouch." Riley stuck her finger in her mouth, sucking the coppery tasting blood from her wound.

Her papa laughed. "Careful there, sweetheart. That one's a little spicy." He checked his watch. "Let's keep moving to the next building. We have no need for these other critters."

Riley popped her finger back out. "What about the chickens?"

"We'll come back for them after awhile. The nice man will hold them for us."

The man behind the table with the birds slapped a "sold" sticker on top of the two purchased cages. They passed by the pigs laying in beds filled with sawdust. The sheep ran back and forth in their pens, always in a tight group, each one circling and pushing toward the center. Riley pointed at the sheep. "Why are they acting that way, Papa?"

"Those are prey creatures. It's their natural instinct to want to be in the center of the flock. That way, they are the most protected. If you watch closely, you'll notice they always keep the youngest in the dead center of the flock."

The sheep continued to push and shove each other, each vying for the best position. Papa motioned Riley onward and into the next building.

Building three had all the big livestock. Riley raised herself on her tiptoes to peek through a small window. A draft horse, with wisps of white hair lining its hooves, kicked the wooden door. Papa reached out and pulled Riley toward him. "Stay back from the door. We don't know how wild these animals are. Let's check out the cattle."

Papa pointed at a small black Angus steer. "Now, there's a couple things to point out. Check for conformation. You want to make sure they are standing on all four legs evenly and not lame."

Riley paced up and down the stalls, peaking in at each and every beast. Most of the cattle stood staring off into the distance, chewing their cud.

Her papa continued. "Check for muscling in the meat breeds. The more muscle the better. Some varieties have double muscling, which is a plus."

Riley paused at a black and white spotted cow. "What about the milk breeds?"

"Check for udder conformation. You want to make sure it's normal size and shape. You've seen enough of our cows to know what's good."

One particular steer standing in his pen stared straight back at her. He didn't look scared or angry. He just watched her closely.

"And the most important factor, always look at the eyes. You get one that makes too much eye contact, and you got a problem. That's a sign of them challenging you. There ain't no way to break a beast like that. Then you got the ones who won't look at you at all. That means they're too scared to be of any use."

Riley continued to gaze at the steer that stared straight back.

Her papa looked at his watch. "Come on, now. Time for us to head into the auction."

Riley followed her papa to the next building. Its doors were shut, and a sign hung on the front that read, "Auction at 3 p.m. Ticket members only." Riley wondered what that meant and where they would get these so-called tickets. Papa knocked twice on the door.

The door cracked open. He pulled out two tickets from his wallet and handed them through the crack in the door. After a moment, the door opened further to allow them both to enter.

All the shades were drawn inside this building, the lights dimmed. Sand covered the floor. They walked across the ground and over to the side where metal bleachers awaited them. They climbed a few rows up and sat to face the center of the building, joining a few folks that arrived early. Below them was a show ring, the type that Riley saw on television. It reminded her of the circus, only this one had more gates. A large chute system for herding livestock led from the far corner of the room all the way to the center of the ring.

A short man waddled to the front of the stands. One blind opened so a stream of sunlight broke through and illuminated him. He raised his voice and shouted to the crowd, welcoming all patrons and mentioning that all bidding should be held until all the animals were introduced.

A whistle blew, and the light shifted toward the back corner of the room. One by one, the animals entered the chute forming a single-file line, each one bumping against the other one. Large colored banners with numbers were pinned onto their flesh. They followed the winding twists and turns until they arrived in the center of the ring. The auctioneer stood to meet them, directing the animals so they formed a continuous circle around him. He held out an electric prod toward the beasts, threatening those that slowed their pace.

Papa held a booklet in his hand and passed it to Riley. Inside was a listing of all animals showcased in the auction next to their colored picture. A list of stats included everything from birthday, sex, parent's heritage, height, and weight. Some of the seasoned stock had previous work experience.

Papa pointed to the book. "Read through that and pick the best one."

She flipped the pages. "Male or female?"

"Well, the one I had to put down was male, so pick one of them. There are still one or two females left in the barn waiting for training. Prior work experience is a must. We're looking for another milker."

One creature stood tall in the ring. His dark hair was slicked back, and his tanned skin glowed against the spotlight. He had good muscling and sound conformation. Riley flipped through the booklet until she found his number, twenty-seven, and read his stats. He worked for a large dairy farm a few counties over for five years. He was familiar with Herringbone style parlors and also had experience transitioning another farm over to robotic milking. Both his parents were born in Mexico.

Riley watched his eyes. He kept his head held high, unlike some of the others that stared at the dirt. He kept eye contact with the announcer in the center of the ring.

Riley pointed straight at him. "Number twenty-seven. That's the one."

Papa grabbed the booklet from his daughter and read over the stats. "Looks good to me. Although, he may be a little too confident. He almost holds too much direct eye contact. We may have to leave him in the barn a little longer before we set him to work. Remember Riley, don't let him out, no matter how nice he may seem. I don't want to have to make another trip back up here next week."

The announcer finished. "We'll start the bidding for number twenty-seven. Do I have $200?"

Papa raised his hand. Another bidder raised his hand. Riley watched the look in her papa's eyes, his mouth was clenched, and his jaw was firm. She had seen that look of determination many times before. They were going home with twenty-seven.

The back and forth continued until the other bidder gave up. The announcer shouted out. "That's $350 going once? Twice? Sold, to the man with his daughter. Feel free to pull your trailer around to the back of the building for loading."

Riley followed Papa out of the building to where they were parked. They first stopped and loaded up the chickens, securing them so they wouldn't slide around on the drive home. Then they pulled up to the back of building four. Riley jumped out of the truck, eager to help.

Her papa followed. "Stay back until I get him loaded."

Papa undid the back latch of the trailer. A few helpers were nearby to make sure number twenty-seven didn't make a break for it. Papa guided the creature into his cage and secured the lock before speaking to him. "Now, do you speak any English?"

The man stared back into Papa's eyes and answered, "*Sí.*"

)O)O(X)O)O(X)O)O(X)X

About the Author

Brooke Reynolds is a veterinarian from Charlotte, North Carolina. When she isn't saving animals, she enjoys writing fiction. Her stories have appeared at such online and print markets as *Massacre Magazine, Fantasia Divinity, The Airgonaut, The Literary Hatchet, Ghost Parachute, Every Day Fiction, Ricky's Back Yard,* and *Coffin Bell.* Her story "Dr. Google" won second place in the 2016 Short Story Contest for Channillo, and her story "Bang Bang" was runner up for the 2018 Flash Fiction Suite Contest at Defenestrationism. You can follow her on twitter @psubamit or check out her website reynoldswrites.org

GUEST EDITOR

Tamela J. Ritter

Tamela J. Ritter's writing has been featured online and in print in *Outside In, The Fandom Universe, The Mary Sue, Piedmont Literary Anthology, Ink Stains, Every Other Thing, Ripple Effect*—where her story "Lucy Too" was nominated for a Pushcart Prize—and *Musings*, where her short stories "Allen Quinn" and "Less Than a Dollar a Day" won Best Fiction two years in a row.

Her first—and hopefully not last—novel, *From These Ashes,* was published in 2013 by Vagabondage Press' Battered Suitcase imprint.

Behind the scenes, she has worked as editor, publisher, and slush pile reader for Vagabondage Press' Dark Alley Press and Battered Suitcase imprints, *Whatever Literary Journal,* and Tears of the Phoenix, a literary charity that raised money for organizations such as the libraries of New Orleans after Hurricane Katrina.

When she's not busy plotting, writing, blogging, and slush pile reading, she can be found baby wrangling in Northern Virginia and planning her next adventure in her quest to travel the world.

See how it all began.

Download your FREE copy of Vol. 1 today, wherever ebooks are sold!

AUTHORS WANTED FOR

INK STAINS ANTHOLOGIES

We are looking for unique dark fiction submissions for upcoming editions of *Ink Stains Anthology* from Dark Alley Press.

Submissions are now open for pieces 3,000-15,0000 words for all works that fit under the Dark Alley Press banner, including those in the following categories:

- Dark fiction (including lit fic)
- Gothic fiction
- Supernatural/paranormal fiction
- Horror
- Steampunk
- Black Comedy
- Fantasy

Authors of acquired pieces for Ink Stains Anthology will receive a flat fee payment upon publication. For more information, check out our website.

www.inkstainsanthology.com